CRYPTID COUNTRY

GERRY GRIFFITHS

SEVERED PRESS
HOBART TASMANIA

CRYPTID COUNTRY

WWW.SEVEREDPRESS.COM

ISBN: 978-1-925840-81-0

DEDICATION

For Auntie Paula

1

HIJACKED

Professor Nora Howard watched the FBI agent—who reminded her so much of the actor Vince Vaughn—march Dr. Joel McCabe away in handcuffs through the crowded airport terminal.

"This way," said another agent, motioning for Nora to follow him. They walked over to a security door behind a ticket counter. The agent swiped an access card in the reader and the door swished open. A narrow corridor led to a flight of stairs to the ground floor. Once at the bottom, the agent used his card to open the door to the outside area.

A black sedan was parked under the nose of a cargo aircraft.

Jack Tremens, Miguel Walla, and an FBI agent stood by a loader lifting a large animal cage out the side door of the plane's cargo hold. More cages were lined up on the tarmac waiting to be transferred inside the back of a white 26-foot moving truck with *Wilde Enterprises* on the sides.

Nora heard an engine approaching.

A Ford Expedition pulled up alongside the car. The front doors opened. Lucas Finder, Carter Wilde's top executive and Cryptid Zoo project manager, got out the passenger-side. The driver was Ivan Connors, head of security for Wilde Enterprises.

The FBI agent went over to talk to the two men.

"How are they doing?" Nora asked Jack.

"Apart from being a little scared, they seem okay."

Nora crouched and looked through the bars at the black mngwa kitten curled up next to the blue tiger kitten, both shivering in the blustering cold.

She peeked in the next cage. The Bergman's bear cub was considerably larger than the felines; three times their size, even though they were created in the laboratory at relatively the same time. It was inconceivable to think the thirty-pound cub would one day weigh over 4,000 pounds and stand sixteen feet tall.

Loud screeches sounded from the cage being lowered to the ground. Two thunderbird chicks squabbled as they were jostled about. Jet-black, they looked like a pair of bookend ravens. Full grown, the birds would be the size of F-14 fighter jets.

Nora heard an animal huff and moved over to the next wire enclosure. A baby bigfoot stared out at her, its misty breath puffing out from between its trembling lips. It stood about three feet tall, its body covered with a thin fine coat that would become thicker and coarse as it approached adulthood. The Sasquatch poked a black finger through the bars. Nora reassured the shivering animal by stroking its finger. "Don't worry, you'll be somewhere warm and safe soon."

She stepped over to a wooden crate with the lid partially pulled back and saw two sauropods resembling miniature brontosauruses the size of Labrador retrievers. The cold-blooded infants showed no signs of discomfort from the chilly temperature.

In one cage, four chupacabras hissed, clinging to the bars with their two-talon claws. They looked like skinned rats with hunched shoulders, standing on their hind legs, their long tails curled like hooks. Their creepy fish eyes were set in egg-shaped heads, mouths agape with cat-like teeth.

Two airport employees worked inside the truck, securing the cages.

The cryptids screeched and wailed.

It was enough to break Nora's heart. And to think, Dr. McCabe might have gotten away and sold them to the highest bidder if she hadn't the forethought of tagging each creature with a mobile tracking device chip.

Once the plane was completely offloaded and the creatures were onboard the truck, the freight handlers climbed out of the vehicle, closing the rear door.

The FBI agent walked back with Finder and Connors.

"I should ride along to make sure they're okay," Nora said to the agent.

"Well, that's not up for me to decide. Officially, I'm done here." He backed away and headed for his car.

Nora looked at Finder.

"I'm afraid I can't let you do that." He reached inside his suit jacket and pulled out two envelopes. He handed Jack and Miguel each an envelope.

"What's this?" Jack asked.

"It's your final checks. Your services will no longer be needed."

Jack looked over at Miguel. "Looks like our cryptid hunting days are over."

"Fine by me." Miguel ran his finger under the seal and opened his envelope. He removed the check. "Are you kidding me?"

Jack opened his and stared at the amount. "The guy's one of the richest men alive and this is all he could cough up after we risked our necks for his damn zoo."

"Carter Wilde prides himself as being a frugal businessman," Finder said.

Miguel clenched his fists and took a step like he might punch the man. "Cheap bastard."

"Back away," Connors said, his hand resting on the butt of his sidearm.

"Oh, I get it," Jack said. "Everything goes to shit and now your boss wants nothing to do with us."

"What about me?" Nora asked Finder. "Surely he'll let me continue my research."

"To tell you the truth, I'm not sure."

"But I need the medical insurance for my mother. I can't afford her treatment. She'll die without it. Please, you have to—"

"We're through here," Connors said.

Jack motioned to the truck. "What about them?"

"What about them? No longer your problem." Connors waved his hand, signaling the truck to leave. He escorted Finder back to their vehicle.

Nora broke down. "Oh, Jack, tell me this isn't happening."

Jack put his arm around her. "Come on, let's get out of here."

They went back inside to the main terminal and made a beeline for the airport lounge. Passengers on standby or delayed due to cancellations occupied the tables and booths.

They managed to find three seats together at the bar with a good view of a big-screen TV mounted high on the wall.

A harried-looking bartender took their drink orders.

Nora glanced up at the large screen, which was playing a golf match but then cut to a live news broadcast of an aerial view taken from a helicopter flying over a massive blue dome structure in the middle of a forest. She flagged down the bartender. "Could you please turn that up?"

The bartender pointed the remote at the TV. "...Our Channel 8 News Chopper is currently on the scene over what is being called Cryptid Zoo; where mysterious creatures have escaped after killing guests at the theme park. It is not known what these creatures are exactly, only that they are extremely dangerous. We will keep you updated, as more information is made available. And now back to our regular programming."

The screen changed to a golfer straddling the ball, ready to tee off.

Nora looked at Jack. "We can't let Wilde get away with this."

"The way I see it, there's not much we can do."

"Yes, there is. But we have to do something first."

"Oh yeah, and what's that?" Jack asked, glancing at Miguel.

"We're going to have to go back to the zoo," she said.

2

THE DOME

The moonlight shimmered through the trees.

Miguel turned off the headlights. He edged the truck onto the shoulder of the dirt road and parked behind a stand of scrub brush. The dashboard clock read 2:35 a.m. when he shut off the engine.

Miguel turned to Nora, sitting between him and Jack. "You really think he's still in there?"

"He's there."

"I don't know," Jack said. "The FBI did a thorough search of the zoo."

"Believe me, he's there."

"Let's hope so." Jack opened the passenger door and climbed out.

Nora and Miguel got out of the truck.

They started up the road on foot, ready to duck for cover in the trees if a car came.

A break in the woods and the massive dome came into view, the turquoise roof covering the gigantic stadium glinting in the moonlight. It looked absurd, and so out of place in the conifers, like an alien spaceship from another planet.

Jack spotted a black sedan and three white *Wilde Enterprises* moving vans parked by the helipad clearing. "Looks like we're going to have company." He turned to Nora. "Sure you want to do this?"

"Jack, I won't leave him in there."

"You do know, once we do this, he'll come after us."

"Let him. I'm not afraid of Carter Wilde."

"Jack's right, Nora," Miguel said. "There'll be no turning back."

Nora gave them a resolved look.

"Okay," Jack said. "I guess we're doing this."

They strode toward the vehicles.

"You know," Miguel said. "He's not going to fit in the bed of my truck. Maybe we could commandeer one of the vans."

Jack opened the driver's door on the nearest van and leaned in. "We're in luck. Keys are in the ignition." He removed the keys and stuffed them in his jacket pocket.

They continued on to the main entrance.

A single spotlight shone on the looming wrought iron archway—*WELCOME TO CRYPTID ZOO*—the rendered doors ripped from their hinges and on the ground.

Jack, Nora, and Miguel stepped inside the dome.

A broad flagstone pathway stretched a short distance between two rows of pedestals and toppled statues to a five-story glass-front hotel. The building seemed vacated except for a single light shining behind a curtained window on the second floor.

The main lobby was dimly lit.

"Oh my God." Nora covered her nose with a scarf.

"It's ammonia." Jack pulled the handkerchief knotted on his neck up around his nose and mouth. Miguel covered his lower face with his handkerchief.

They stepped down the slimy walkway, avoiding the decomposing fish swept out of the Tank after the 900,000-gallon aquarium ruptured. It was like walking on a debris-strewn beach after a tsunami. Jack skirted a bloated grouper crawling with maggots, a smelly decaying leopard shark with no eyes.

To the left was the ZOOKEEPERS & PARK STAFF housing; on the right the SECURITY building. The round two-story structures were dark, except for the outdoor landscaping lighting fixtures illuminating the walkways.

Jack gazed up at the looming 250-foot steel girded ceiling resembling the inside framework of a dirigible.

"Get down. Someone's coming." Miguel motioned toward a bronze statue of a giant black panther lying on its side. Jack and Nora hid alongside Miguel.

A security guard walked patrol by the hotel. He wore black tactical gear and carried an assault rifle.

"That's not FBI," Miguel whispered. "That's one of Connors' men."

Jack glanced over at Nora. "Which means we better be extra careful. They spot us they won't think twice about shooting."

Jack gazed at the Aviary next to the hotel. He spotted the gaping holes in the netting fifty feet above the hotel rooftop created by the gigantic thunderbirds during their escape.

They waited for the guard to disappear between the hotel and the giant flight cage.

"Now." Miguel darted to the left side of the hotel. They stayed low and raced past the lobby windows so as not to be seen even though there didn't appear to be anyone inside. The concrete walkway took them to the Olympic-size swimming pool where they took a moment to hide behind two high stacks of poolside chaise lounges.

The guard appeared from around the corner. He stopped to light a cigarette. He leaned against the wall, enjoying his smoke.

Jack was getting impatient. "Come on," he whispered in a harsh tone.

Flicking the butt into the pool, the guard turned and went back the way he had come.

Miguel jumped up. "Let's go."

Jack and Nora dashed after Miguel down an aggregate pathway to a round building behind the hotel. The sign over the entry—BIO-ENGINNERING LABORATORY AND ANIMATRONICS WORKSHOP COMPLEX—readable in the glow of the outdoor lights staked in the flowerbed bordering the front entrance.

They entered the building, rushing through a foyer past a doorway to an auditorium. Heading down a long corridor, the three passed the laboratory where Nora and Dr. Joel McCabe had created the cryptid specimens for the zoo.

Jack saw the door to the Animatronics Workshop had been left open. He took a quick glance inside. The room was empty. Burt Owen, Hollywood's legendary special effects wizard responsible for the designs and creating some of the robotic creatures displayed in the zoo, had cleared out his equipment.

Miguel pushed through the exit door, taking them outside down a walkway to another building: BIPED HABITAT. Jack and Nora followed Miguel inside. Only a few auxiliary lights remained on. They hurried down a hallway to the center of the building and stood in the middle of an atrium with five separate habitats, each twenty feet wide and extending back sixty feet in a pie wedge floor plan.

The entry doors stood open.

Each habitat had a different theme: a redwood forest; a snowcapped mountain ridge; a sand and cacti desert; a rumpus room with tractor tires and monkey bars.

The thick viewing window had been smashed from the jungle exhibit. Jagged glass and shards littered the blood-smeared floor.

Nora entered the habitat. She parted the foliage and entered the faux jungle.

Jack and Miguel kept watch as Nora searched the enclosure.

After waiting a couple of minutes, Jack called out, "Anything?"

Nora came out of the bushes. “No. I looked everywhere.”

“Then we better—”

“Hold it right there.” A security guard came down the hall, pointing his carbine.

Jack and Miguel turned. They threw up their hands.

“One move and you’re dead.”

“We can explain.” Nora began to step down.

“I said—” The guard was picked up off his feet and slammed against the wall.

Jack went over and knelt beside the man slumped on the floor. “He’s out cold but he’s still breathing.”

“Thank God,” Nora said.

The three looked up at the towering figure standing in the middle of the hall.

Nora smiled. “Hello, Lennie.”

3

ROSIE

SIX MONTHS LATER...

Miguel took down the pump-action hanging on the wall over the header of the backdoor. He slipped three 12-guage cartridges one at a time past the tang then pulled back the slide to insert a shell into the shotgun's chamber.

"Would you like a pastrami and Swiss sandwich?" Maria asked, standing at the kitchen counter, preparing Sophia's school lunch for tomorrow. She had on Miguel's Fleetwood Mac T-shirt, a baggy pair of her green striped pajama bottoms, thick booty socks, and still looked sexy.

"What, we're out of liverwurst?" Miguel peered out through the kitchen curtains.

"I'm afraid so." Maria made a face as she spread mayonnaise on slices of bread arranged on the cutting board. "I don't know how you can eat that stuff."

Miguel continued to gaze out behind the house. "Not my fault you haven't acquired a taste for it."

"Just like you'll never catch me eating beets or lima beans."

"Your loss."

The family's black Lab, Rosie, was sitting anxiously by Miguel's feet. She gazed up at Miguel and whined.

"Miguel, she needs to go out."

"I know, just give me a second to make sure." Miguel strained to see the edge of the woods behind the house. He had rigged motion detectors in the trees bordering the small clearing serving as their backyard with wooden armchairs, a picnic table, a fire pit, and a brick-enclosed barbeque Miguel had built himself with his limited masonry skills.

So far, the floodlights hadn't come on.

"Miguel, she really has to pee."

Rosie remained on her rump, squirming closer to the door.

Miguel looked down at Rosie's pleading face. She was two months along and due to deliver anytime soon, her teats swollen on her bulging belly. She looked ready to burst. "Okay, okay." He unlocked the door and pushed it open ever so slowly.

He stepped out onto the back deck, activating the porch lights. He glanced around at the top of the steps. A half-moon was visible through the treetops. He could feel a cool pine-scented breeze on his face. The edge of the forest was a wall of shadows and sharp-edged silhouettes.

"Rosie!" Miguel called out just above a whisper as he went down the stairs. "Come, girl!" He could hear her thumping down the steps behind him. He kept a vigilant watch on the woods.

A branch cracked somewhere in the darkness.

Miguel raised the barrel of the shotgun in the direction of the noise.

A scream came from inside the house.

It was his daughter, Sophia.

Miguel spun around to face the back door. "Maria! What's she screaming about?"

Maria came to the doorway. Sophia had run from her bedroom and was clinging to her mother. "She saw something out her window."

"Jesus," Miguel cursed. He stepped to the corner of the house and looked down the wood siding to Sophia's bedroom window where the hallway light was shining through her room. He heard rustling in the shrub oak. Something was definitely lurking out in the bushes. Prowling around the house.

It sounded big by its movements. And for that he blamed himself. After all, if it hadn't been for him and his best friend, Jack Tremens, those things wouldn't be out there scouring the countryside. He could kick himself until doomsday but that wasn't going to change anything. His only concern right now was making sure his family was safe.

Miguel rushed back to the bottom porch step and looked up. "Close the door."

"Where's Rosie?" Maria pulled Sophia behind her.

"Rosie!" Miguel yelled. He blew out a high-pitched whistle. He scanned the edge of the forest but it was impossible to spot her black coat in the dark. "Rosie, here girl!"

Miguel heard a branch snap.

The floodlights triggered on.

An eight-foot tall figure stood at the outmost rim of the light.

Miguel stood fast with the shotgun ready.

The creature retreated back into the moonlit thicket.

Heavy footfalls raced up the side of the house. A flashlight beam caught Miguel directly in the face. He put up his hand to shield his eyes.

"I heard yelling. Everything okay?"

"Yeah, hey Bron."

Bron Banner lived a short distance down the road with his wife, Betsy, and their daughter, Tess. Like all neighbors living in the rural community, everyone looked out for each other and was always there to assist in the event of trouble.

Miguel's heart sunk when he saw something lying on the ground near the edge of the woods. "Bron, shine your flashlight over there." Miguel pointed at the lump on the ground.

The flashlight's beam shone on a dead animal lying in the dirt.

"Oh, God no." Miguel started to approach.

"Miguel? What's wrong?" Maria stepped out onto the porch.

Bron kept the light shining on the unrecognizable shape.

Maria rushed down the steps in her stockinged feet. "Rosie!" She ran past Miguel who tried to stop her but she pulled away. Miguel and Bron hurried after her.

Miguel grabbed Maria by the arm and looked down. He could see the mutilated head where the snout had been bitten off, the eyes gouged, the neck snapped back severing the spine. The right front leg had been ripped off. The belly was split open.

Maria collapsed into Miguel's arms. "Thank God."

"You don't see many black wolves in these parts," Bron said. He looked at Maria who was wiping the tears from her cheeks. "Did you think that was Rosie?"

A familiar bark sounded in the dark.

Miguel turned. Two large dogs trotted into the yard.

It was Rosie and Bron's yellow Lab, Gunther.

Dropping to her knees, Maria beckoned Rosie over. She gave the dog a big hug around the neck and kissed the crown of her head. "Rosie, you silly, don't scare us like that." Rosie licked Maria's face as if to apologize for making her worry. Maria stood. She shooed the pregnant dog up the steps and followed her into the house.

The timer turned off the floodlights.

Bron shined his flashlight into the trees. "Remember when it was safe to go out at night and not have to worry?"

"Not really."

"They've decided to reopen the Blue Ridge campground." Bron was a park ranger for the US Forest Service. The campground had been closed due to a savage attack on some campers by an unidentified wild animal.

"Not a good idea but I guess you can't keep it closed forever," Miguel said.

Bron looked at the dead wolf. “Think it was the bigfoot?”

“Yeah.” Miguel saw Maria standing at the kitchen window, waiting for him to come inside. He looked at Bron. “Thanks for coming over.”

“That’s what neighbors do. Watch each others’ backs.”

“See you tomorrow.”

Bron gave Gunther a short whistle and they headed home.

Miguel came back inside the house and locked the door. He unloaded the shotgun and hung it back on the wall. He turned off the kitchen light. He checked in on Sophia to make sure she was okay. She was fast asleep.

Rosie was curled beside Sophia’s bed. The dog raised her head to acknowledge Miguel then plopped down on the thick weave throw rug.

Miguel left the bedroom door open a crack so the hall light could filter in as a nightlight. He went down the hall.

Maria was waiting for him in their bed.

He took off his boots and stripped out of his clothes.

“Still no word from Jack?” Maria asked.

“No. He knows better than to try and contact us directly.”

“I really worry about him.”

“Me too.”

“Nothing on the website?”

“That would be the first place they would look. I’ve posted that the Cryptid Hunters are officially on hiatus.”

“But you’re still putting out the word?”

“Warning folks, you bet. I can’t help feeling partly responsible.”

“You didn’t know.”

Miguel switched off the lamp on the nightstand and crawled under the covers. He placed his arm over Maria’s shoulder, pulling her tight against his body. He hoped he could sleep. Lately, it was impossible to get a good night’s rest knowing there were those creatures out there in the woods, watching the house.

Maria reached back and gave Miguel’s hip a squeeze. “Don’t let Sophia see that poor animal.”

“I’ll get up early and bury it in the woods.”

4

LENNIE

Jack brought the blade down and cleaved the short log in two. He buried the ax head into the stump. He leaned over, collecting an armful of split wood. As he stood, he cocked his head, listening to the sounds all around him. The rustling branches in the tall pines, the distant keen of a predatory bird, the otherwise quiet of the remote Pacific Northwest Forest. Just the way he liked it.

He carried the firewood over to the rustic cabin; the sloped roof covered with a thin brown blanket of pine needles. He placed the split wood neatly on the already made stack by the front door. He brushed off his hands, stomped the dirt from his boots, and went inside.

The interior was one large room with a moderate-sized bed tucked against one wall under the window. The door to the wardrobe cabinet was partially open revealing the hung clothes and drawers. Two footlockers were positioned in the center of the space between a pair of matching rocking chairs facing the stone hearth.

A rug was bunched by the raised lid of the trapdoor leaned back on its hinges, flat on the floor. Jack glanced down in the root cellar. He went down a few steps. As it was much cooler underground, the cellar served as an excellent pantry for keeping provisions, plus there was the emergency evacuation escape tunnel. He came back up the steps, closed the trapdoor, and covered the hatch with the rug.

"You really shouldn't leave that open," Jack said to Nora sitting in the compact kitchen area with its four-legged wash basin for cleaning dishes and a wood burning stove used for cooking and heating the cabin.

It seemed strange watching her rolling flat dough back and forth on the flour-covered tabletop like a pioneer woman in her denim shirt and blue jeans when only six months ago the renowned geneticist and cryptozoologist wouldn't be caught dead out of her white lab coat.

She looked up and gave Jack a smile. "Sorry, I needed some preservatives and forgot to close it."

"Sure would hate to walk in and break my neck."

"We wouldn't want that. After I put this in the pan to rise, do you want to go down to the creek?"

"Might be a good time to check the nets." Normally Jack would have preferred using a fishing pole, but that would have been a tedious method feeding a creature with an insatiable appetite that could consume a hundred pounds of fish, fruit, and leaves in a single meal.

Also, it would have meant Jack sitting on the bank in plain sight and running the risk of being spotted by a passing search plane.

As much as Jack hated to admit it, he and Nora were fugitives. They had possession of what Carter Wilde believed to be his patented property; the CEO and owner of the largest conglomerate of incorporated high-tech organizations in the world under the umbrella of Wilde Enterprises.

Shortly after the Cryptid Zoo calamity, Wilde had done everything in his power to separate himself from the tragedy, even denying Nora's mother's medical treatments which resulted in her passing only days after Nora and Jack rescued and ran off with Lennie. Afraid that Wilde's men would be waiting to nab her at the funeral, Nora never got the chance to say a proper farewell to her mother, further fueling her hatred for Carter Wilde.

Jack and Nora donned their coats and went outside. They walked around the side of the cabin and followed the path down through the trees to the water's edge. The glacial mountain run-off cascading down the bedrock and skimming over the standing pools tucked in the rocky coves had swollen the creek into a fast-moving stream.

A fallen Douglas fir stretched across the swift current to the other side of the shore.

Jack gazed out at the large boulder in the middle of the stream he used to benchmark the water levels, noticing a new watermark higher up the rock. "It's risen since yesterday." He knew it would be a challenge in the deeper water, unhooking the nets strung out on the main line attached to the bottom of the massive log connecting to the opposite bank.

A three-foot long sockeye salmon leaped out of the water, jockeying its way upstream. The pristine roiling water was teeming with migratory red fish, the abundant salmon run like being handed a free shopping spree at a supermarket. He sprinted over to the end of the Douglas fir where the heavy tree had uprooted out of the ground. He climbed up on the four-foot wide curved trunk with jutting branches serving as handholds whenever crossing to the other side.

He went out twenty feet and knelt on the bark. He leaned over, grabbing a draw line that would enable him to close up a net to capture the fish. As he strained to pull up the rope, he quickly realized the net was completely full with over ten thrashing salmon; each fish weighing up to fifteen pounds.

"Jack, be careful!" Nora hollered from the bank.

He put his back into it and tried to lift the net out of the water. His knees slipped on the damp bark. He felt himself sliding off and let go of the line but it was too late to prevent him from falling into the water. He clung onto the top rope secured to the tree. He tried standing on the creek bottom. Each time his boots touched the gravel, the soles would slip out from under him or a strong swimming salmon would batter his legs.

He considered trying to make for the shore. He pushed off the underside of the log but didn't get far as his boot got entangled in the netting. He grabbed hold of a branch so as not to be swept underwater. Jack reached for his knife sheathed on his belt. Even if he cut himself loose, there was a good chance he would be swept downstream to where whitewater rapids churned a mile away down a steep-wall canyon.

Jack went under and came back up. Gasping for air, he shot a glance at the shore. Nora was climbing onto the fallen tree. He watched as she made her way toward the spot where he had fallen off.

"Hang on Jack!" Nora yelled. She got down on her belly and extended her hand.

"There's no way you can pull me up." Jack held onto the rope but didn't offer his hand for fear he might yank Nora into the water. He watched Nora duck out of sight for a moment then return with another length of rope.

"I've tied the end off. Grab hold and see if you can pull yourself up." Nora tossed down the line.

Jack snatched the rope and held on. He dipped down in the water with his knife and cut his boot free from the netting. He kicked his feet to propel upward. Nora leaned down to help him.

"Oh, no..." Nora tumbled down, splashing into the fast-moving current.

Jack fell back down and reached out to save her but she was swept under the log. "NORA!" He gazed down the swift moving creek but couldn't see her as the turbulent waters reached a bend in the trees and elbowed from view.

His arms grew tired from clinging to the rope and being tossed about by the strong current. He heard heavy stomping overhead and looked up.

A giant furry hand reached down, snatching him out of the water. He was carried away like an infant tucked under a parent's arm.

Once on the bank, Jack was released to fall onto the pebbled shore. "Ouch, thanks." He saw Nora sitting on a rock, sopping wet but alive.

"Good thing you called out my name when you did," Nora said, wringing out the bottom of her shirt. "Sure got Lennie's attention."

Jack stared up at the twelve-foot tall yeren better known as the Chinese wildman, a larger version of the North American bigfoot. The dopey-looking cryptid resembled a giant orangutan with its long orangey-brown hair and elongated body that looked like it had been stretched twice its size on a torturer's rack. Lennie gazed down at Jack and flapped its black lips like a horse, blowing him a raspberry.

"Very funny." Jack got to his feet. Standing next to the yeren, Jack was always amazed at its great size, its arms as long as Jack was tall; and he was six-foot.

Lennie ambled up to Nora, touching her gently on the shoulder. There was a strong bond between the geneticist that assisted in creating the cryptid and the beast for its co-creator.

Nora squeezed one of Lennie's fingers, which was as big as her hand. "If you're hungry, there's a nice catch waiting." She pointed at the nets strung out under the log. Lennie understood and waded out into the creek, the swift-moving water only up to his thighs. The yeren grabbed a net full of salmon. He dragged it onto the shore away from the water's edge.

Lennie sat on the bank with his legs extended like a big kid. He grabbed a fifteen-pound sockeye with one meaty hand and bit it in half. Some of the floundering salmon tried to wriggle out of the net. Lennie scooped up the ones that got out, chomping on them so they wouldn't get away. The yeren was a gluttonous eating machine.

"Are we just going to sit here watching him eat?" Jack asked Nora.

"No, we could be here for a while. Let's go back to the cabin. I want to get out of these wet clothes."

"I'm all for that."

"Yeah, I bet you are."

"You know, I don't always have a one-track mind." Jack and Nora could only be intimate when Lennie was distracted away from the cabin. The one time the big apeman happened to peek through the cabin window and saw Jack and Nora having sex, the cryptid went ballistic and almost killed Jack, thinking he was hurting her.

"Jack, you're about as—"

Jack raised his hand to silence Nora when he heard a distant whirling sound. He glanced over at Lennie. The yeren was already gone like a puff of smoke. Jack hadn't even heard the big creature leave. For being such a large animal, it had the uncanny ability to disappear in the blink of an eye.

"The trees." Jack grabbed Nora's hand and they dashed into the forest. They quickly got down behind a thick bush. Jack spread the branches apart so he could see the creek. He could hear the whine of a small motor. A black object with four propeller blades flew along the shoreline of the stream.

The unmanned aerial vehicle hovered above the fallen log for a moment then drifted over to the bank where the salmon flopped on the gravel in an attempt to escape the net.

"What is it?" Nora whispered, unable to see through the brush.

"It's a drone." Jack watched the small aircraft make a pattern search of the area. One time it headed straight to where they were hiding. Jack had to duck back behind the bush. He prayed the cameras on the drone hadn't picked up his movement.

It stayed for another few minutes then soared off down the creek.

"Do you think it saw us?" Nora asked.

"I don't think so."

* * *

Ivan Connors watched his three pilots toggling their control pads while they stared at the aerial views on their computer screens. The stiff bench seat in the mobile drone command center was killing his back. As head of security for Wilde Enterprises it was important for him to go out in the field when need be, even if it meant having to micro-manage his various teams protecting the interests of the vast parent corporation.

"Sir, you might want to look at this," a drone pilot said, his eyes not wavering from his screen.

"What do you have?" Connors replied, glad to finally be standing. He stepped behind the operator who zoomed in on the image.

Large red fish floundered on the bank of a creek.

"So? There're salmon. They must have jumped out of the water."

"No, sir. Take a closer look. They're trying to get out of a net."

Connors leaned in closer. Damn, he was right. He patted the operator on the shoulder. "Good job."

Stepping to the front of the vehicle, Connors sat in the contoured front passenger seat. He took his satellite phone out of his pocket and punched in a speed number. He waited for a few seconds then said, "Get your men ready. I'll have one of my operators send you the coordinates." Connors ended the call.

A gratifying smile came over his face. "Gotcha."

5

ON THE AIR

Lucas Finder was wishing he hadn't let his boss, Carter Wilde bamboozle him into guest appearing on The Marty Mayer Show to promote the billionaire's latest extravaganza.

He was becoming irritated with the make-up girl. She was doing her best to mask the sheen on his face and kept flicking the fine powder in his eyes. Finally, he'd had enough and put up his hand. "I think I'm glamorous enough."

"But I'm not—"

Lucas slipped off the canvas chair, removing the cloth draped over his shoulders meant to protect his suit jacket. He looked down and noticed a smudge on his lapel. He licked his finger, rubbed the blemish, which only made it more prominent.

"Mr. Finder, we'll need to get you prepped during the commercial break." A harried young man carrying a clipboard and wearing a wireless headset with a tiny microphone motioned for Lucas to follow him.

Lucas made sure not to trip over the cables strewn on the floor like black pythons. They went over to a curtain partially pulled back. Looking over his shoulder, Lucas couldn't believe the hectic backstage activity; the crew scrambling like a buzzing beehive making sure everything was right on schedule and went off without a hitch.

"Let's get you seated." The young man escorted Lucas onto the large stage.

Two hundred people sat in five tiered rows of twenty seats split down the middle with an aisle of steps leading up to an exit door. A young woman with a microphone was standing in front of the stage, warming up the audience and had just finished a story that had everyone laughing.

As Lucas walked over to the interviewee chair next to Marty Mayer's desk, he could hear the woman instructing everyone to pay attention to the applaud sign when it lit up and the proper time to join in when they heard the recorded canned laughter whenever Marty made one of his corny jokes.

Marty Mayer was nowhere to be seen.

Lucas figured he was backstage sneaking a cigarette. He sat down in the chair while a sound technician attached a small microphone just above his tie clip.

A voice did a countdown from ten over a loud speaker. By the time it came to five, Marty Mayer was scurrying onto the stage. He plopped in his chair behind his desk just as the camera lights came on and a big screen suspended at the rear of the stage flashed *Welcome back to The Marty Mayer Show* accompanied by an announcer's introduction and the show's familiar jingle.

Marty smiled at the audience. "Please give a warm welcome for Lucas Finder."

The applaud sign lit up and everyone clapped their hands.

Lucas smiled sheepishly at the crowd.

Marty turned in his chair to face his guest. "Nice you can join us."

"Thanks for inviting me. It's a pleasure to be here," Lucas lied.

"So, I guess congratulations are in order. You are now the Chief Operating Officer of Wilde Enterprises."

Someone in the audience booed.

Marty ignored the heckling and continued by saying, "Tell us about your new project."

Lucas leaned slightly forward in his chair. "We have just completed construction of what will be called Wilde Skyway. Currently the tallest building in the world *was* Burj Khalifa in Dubai, United Arab Emirates, which is 2,722 feet tall."

"And how tall is Wilde Skyway?"

"Our structure is 2,908 feet tall; twelve stories higher than the skyscraper in Dubai. Imagine stacking two Empire State Buildings one on top of the other and you will have Wilde Skyway."

Some of the audience members gasped and muttered with astonishment.

"That is impressive."

"Well, we do have the best architects in the world."

"Oh, I'm sure you have."

"We're looking forward to inauguration day and should have the ceremonial cutting of the ribbon very soon," Lucas boasted.

Marty leaned on his desk and clasped his hands together. "Surely, there has to be limits? I mean, a building more than half a mile in the sky? It must raise some concerns."

"Believe me, Marty. We've taken all precautions."

"Like you did with Cryptid Zoo?"

Lucas bit his lip finding himself suddenly in the hot seat. He glanced out at the audience and saw their rapture stares. He'd hoped the horrific event was old news and long forgotten but there was always someone wanting to dig up the past; and now the hot topic discussion was back on the table. "That was regrettable."

"That's all you have to say: that was regrettable. A lot of people died."

"Yes, that's right," Lucas scrambled. "But Wilde Enterprises wasn't entirely to blame. As you know, Dr. Joel McCabe—"

"This week marks the six-month anniversary since the massacre," Marty said, rudely interrupting Lucas. The host picked up a sheet of paper off his desk. "Before you say anymore, maybe you could explain why Carter Wilde thought his attraction was safe to the general public?"

"We had taken all precautions—"

"And you thought these-" Marty glanced up at the audience knowing the camera was zooming in on his face "-*creatures* were not dangerous."

"No more so than any other animal in a zoo. They were contained."

"Until they weren't." Marty stared at the paper he was holding. "I know there were news reports of the tragic event but perhaps you wouldn't mind elaborating on what really happened."

Lucas could feel the sweat beading on his forehead, ruining his makeup. He wanted nothing better than to rip his mike off and storm off the set but that would have only made matters worse. The reason Carter Wilde wasn't sitting here being grilled was because he expected Lucas to take the bullet for him. Which is how Lucas felt at the moment—like a condemned man standing in front of a firing squad.

Marty Mayer pressed on by saying, "Our research staff has put together quite a list that I would like to share with you and our audience."

"I'm afraid I'm not at liberty to discuss the events that transpired at the Dome."

"Cover-up!" someone shouted from the audience, backed with a chorus of boos.

Lucas glared at Marty hoping the camera wasn't panning in on his scowling face, making him appear hostile. At the moment, he wanted to vault over the desk and rip Marty Mayer's throat out with his bare hands. Maybe he could rationalize his way out of the dilemma.

"It's not that I don't want to be forthright," Lucas said. "I'm bound by a non-disclosure confidential agreement with my employer. If I were to share any knowledge of what happened, the corporate lawyers at Wilde Enterprises would be all over me. To be quite frank, I like my job and want to keep it."

"Fair enough, I understand." Marty took a moment to take a sip from the large mug on his desk. Lucas swore he smelled booze in the coffee.

Marty Mayer gazed at the paper in his hand. "What's a mgnwa? That's a strange name."

"I thought we weren't going to discuss this."

"As you wish. You don't mind if I run down the list and make a stab at it, do you?"

"Be my guest."

Marty looked over at his producer standing just off camera. "Daley, feel free to jump in anytime."

"You got it, Marty," Daley beamed.

"A mngwa according to our researchers is a giant panther-type cat that is the size of a horse. Am I right?" Marty asked Lucas.

"That would be correct."

Marty smiled up at the audience. "This is quite the list." He looked back at the page and started reading off the names. "We have bigfoot, blue tigers, flying snakes called arabhars, ahools..." Marty glanced over at Daley.

"They're megabats. Big megabats."

"Thank you for clarifying. Let's see, there're thunderbirds." Marty looked at Lucas. "Really, thunderbirds? How large are they?"

Lucas figured what the hell. Mayer's researchers had looked the things up on the internet anyway. "About the size of a single engine Cessna."

"Oh my." Marty continued on. "Bergman's bear. Am I reading this right? It stands sixteen feet tall and weighs 4,000 pounds?"

"That sounds about right."

"My God. Mongolian death worms?" Marty's dramatic tone elicited a few awes from the audience. "Bili apes?" Marty looked to Daley for confirmation.

"Sometimes called the Great Lion-Eating Chimp."

Marty looked back at the sheet of paper. "Chinese wildman? What in God's name is a Chinese wildman?"

Lucas saw no harm in adding, "The correct term is yeren. It's a large version of the sasquatch."

Marty scratched his head in disbelief as he rattled off a few more names, pausing at, "Chupacabras? Says here that's Spanish for *goatsucker*. I'm sure the kiddies wouldn't be seeing that one at the petting zoo." He laughed and the audience joined in.

Lucas knew he was being mocked. Marty Mayer had no children. He'd been married three times and each one ended in a bad divorce. The talk show host was paying alimony out his ears and close to bankrupt; at least that was what the tabloids claimed.

Marty composed himself and sat up straight in his chair. He took on a more serious look. “All kidding aside, these are some seriously scary creatures.”

“Which is why Carter Wilde thought they would be big attractions.”

“And now they’re out there running wild, thanks to him.”

The audience’s reaction was that of an angry mob brewing.

“That’s not entirely true. Some were hunted down and destroyed.”

Daley signaled Marty that it was time to wrap up.

“Well, that’s our show for today. Thanks for popping in. This is Marty Mayer hoping you have a bang up day.” Marty sat back in his chair as the stage lights dimmed.

Stagehands came out from behind the curtains to rearrange the set pieces and lighting for a different live show scheduled for later in the day. Ushers pointed people to the nearest exits. Lucas got up and glared at Marty Mayer. “I don’t appreciate being blindsided.”

“Then you shouldn’t have made yourself such an easy target,” Marty said smugly with a sneer.

“Oh yeah? Choke on this.” Ripping his mike off, Lucas dumped it in Marty’s coffee mug and marched off the set.

6

CRYPTID HELL

Nick Wells pressed a button on the remote and switched off the television. "He sure reamed Finder, not that he didn't deserve it."

"You really believe that crap about a non-disclosure agreement?" Meg said.

"I had to sign one," Nick reminded his wife. "But then I no longer work there."

"You don't think they'll come after us?"

"Because of my book? It's time people knew the truth." Nick got up from the couch and paced the room. He walked over to the two cardboard boxes against the wall, filled with his tell-all tale of the nightmarish weekend he, Meg, and their son, Gabe, spent trapped inside the Cryptid Zoo dome with the hellish creatures. Nick took a copy of *CRYPTID HELL* out of the box. He gazed at the book cover like a doting parent and dropped it back with the other paperbacks he planned to take along to his book signing.

Meg grabbed her glass of wine from the coffee table. "I have to say Marty Mayer can be a bit of a dick."

"Yeah, I hope he doesn't rake me over the coals when I'm on his show; still a good way to plug the book. His ratings are through the roof."

"I wish you hadn't sent them an advanced copy."

"Why?"

"I don't want him talking about Gabe."

"Meg, I doubt if Mayer even read the book. That's what they have producers for."

"Our boy's been through enough without being made a mockery on national TV."

"I just wish he'd snap out of it."

"Nick!" Meg gave him a hard stare. "He can't help it. Our son was traumatized."

"I'm sorry. That came out wrong." Nick came back and sat on the couch next to Meg. "It's just that he doesn't seem to be getting any better. Don't you think it makes me ill to see him that way? I just wish the doctors could figure out what's wrong with him."

"It'll take time. We just have to be patient."

"Patient? Oh for God sakes, Meg. It's been six months."

"I know but Doctor Phelps says he's seen mark improvement in Gabe's condition."

"What, that he can feed himself?"

"It shows he's making some progress. Please, let's not argue."

"Well, let's look on the bright side, maybe the book's royalties will help with the medical bills."

Meg furrowed her brow and laughed.

"I know, wishful thinking."

"What do you think really happened to Bob and Rhonda?"

"What do you mean?"

"Do you really believe that cock-and-bull story they fed us about Bob having a heart attack?"

"I don't know. It does seem suspicious."

"Especially the medevac chopper catching fire and crashing."

"I wish we knew what happened to Shawn. First his parents and then he disappears."

"I'll bet anything, he was eaten by one of those things."

They heard something crash from another part of the house.

Meg sat up straight. "What was that?"

"Sounded like it came from the backyard." Nick got up and headed toward the kitchen. Meg followed close behind.

Nick walked over to the sliding glass door. He looked out onto the patio area. A flowerpot had fallen off a table and shattered on the shale leaving a mess of broken pottery and dumped potting soil. Maybe a cat, or a bird; he swore he saw something black dart through the bushes.

"What was it?"

"I don't know. I didn't get a good look. Probably the neighbor's cat." He reached for the handle to unlock the sliding glass door and froze.

"Nick, are you okay? You're shaking."

He looked at his trembling hand.

Jesus, Nick. Get a grip on yourself and quit being so paranoid. It was only a damn cat.

7

GREEN THUMB

Laney Moss scanned the barcode labels on the black plastic pots in the customer's shopping cart. She glanced at the screen on the cash register. "That'll be forty-three dollars and sixty-five cents."

The man opened his billfold. He took out a credit card and started to swipe it in the reader.

"Oh, I'm sorry. It's broken," Laney lied. "Could you pay with cash?"

"Uh, sure." He slid the card back in his wallet and handed her three twenties.

She gave him back his change. "The heavenly bamboo is hearty in the direct sunlight but make sure to give them plenty of water to start out so they root properly."

"Thanks for the tip."

"Always glad to be of help," Laney said with a grin. She watched him push his purchases out to the parking lot. He loaded the plants into his hatchback, leaving the shopping cart near the nursery's entrance. He got in his Subaru and took off down the dirt road through the trees.

Even though the remote location deterred a brisk business, it was essential the nursery be away from mainstream traffic. Tucked in a small canyon, the nearest paved road from the nursery was a short jaunt away, the closest suburban community another five-mile drive.

Laney and her husband, Allen, had acquired the small business a year ago, which also included a cottage in the back of the property, along with a greenhouse where Allen performed his botanical talents.

The nursery was the perfect facade.

A white-haired woman in her mid-seventies entered the nursery with a zip in her step.

Laney gave her a warm smile. "Hello, Alice."

Alice Kendrick returned the smile. "Hello, dear. I was wondering if you might suggest something to liven up my home."

"Oh? What's the occasion?"

A slight blush came over the old woman's cheeks.

"Don't tell me, you have a gentleman friend?" It had been a year since Alice's Walter passed. They'd been married forty-nine years.

"Is it that obvious?"

"Nice to see you happy," Laney said.

"Well, I have you to thank for that."

"How are you feeling?"

"Like a spring chicken."

Laney laughed. "What would you say to an asparagus fern? Maybe peace lilies or a spider plant; if you prefer more color, I can recommend some lovely peacock plants and bromeliads."

"That would be splendid."

"Good. I'll get right on it."

"Thank you, dear."

Laney walked over to the indoor plant section.

She loaded an assortment of six 1-gallon plants into a small wagon and pulled it over to a long table. A trowel and an open bag of potting soil were on the tabletop along with a back row of decorative clay pots. She slipped on her garden gloves.

Alice watched as Laney began transferring each plant from a plastic pot to a clay one. She glanced around making sure there was no one in the nursery. "I know I'm a day early but I was wondering if you might fix me up?"

Laney stopped digging and looked at Alice. "Where'd you hear that expression?"

"Toby."

"Makes me sound like a drug dealer."

Alice giggled. "I suppose it does."

"So I take it Toby's the mysterious beau?" Laney patted the topsoil firmly around the stalk of a spider plant.

"We're friends."

"Seems like you're more than friends."

"Maybe," Alice said with a sly grin.

Laney finished and put the repotted plants in the wagon.

"How much is that?" Alice asked, opening her handbag.

"Call it a housewarming gift."

"You could hardly call it *that*. I've lived in the same house for the past fifty-years."

"I'll be right back." Laney dashed off to her office: a Tuff Shed with electricity, a chair and desk, and some file cabinets.

She unlocked the bottom drawer of the desk.

Inside, twenty plastic Ziploc bags filled with herbs.

She took out a bag and locked the drawer. She went out. "Here you are," she said and handed the bag to Alice.

Alice stared at the bag in her hand like it was the most precious thing in the world.

Her eyes teared up. She looked at Laney. "You're an angel."

"I'm just the messenger. You have Allen to thank."

"And where *is* that husband of yours. How come I never see him?"

"That's 'cause he's always busy puttering around in the greenhouse."

"I sure would love to meet him."

"Sure, maybe someday if I can ever drag him away from his work. How is the tumor?"

"Last X-ray it was nearly gone. Even my doctor is amazed. Of course he insists it's the chemo turning things around but I know better."

"Let me help you out to your car." Laney pulled the wagon out into the parking lot to Alice's Toyota Corolla. She placed the potted plants inside a cardboard flat so they wouldn't slide around behind the backseat.

Alice kissed Laney on the cheek.

Laney watched her friend drive away. She pulled the empty wagon back inside the nursery. It was lunchtime so she closed the gate with the sign posting the business hours and the one-hour break between noon and one.

She walked through the nursery and out the back way. She followed a dirt path to a fork in the trail. She could see the cottage in the trees to her left. She turned right and walked through the maple trees until she reached the front entrance of the greenhouse.

The glass-framed structure stood fifteen feet high and was twenty feet wide, stretching back sixty feet.

The entry door was closed.

Laney turned the handle and pushed open the door; her senses immediately greeted with tantalizing fragrances and cloying humidity, the interior a vibrant flowery motif of exotic foliage like an impressionistic painting by the French artist Georges Pierre Seurat. She heard rustling on both sides of her.

She glanced up at the two man-eating trees looming over her. "Easy boys, it's only me."

The twelve-foot tall trees withdrew their grappling branches that looked like giant skeletal hands. They closed their gaping maws; menacing woody-spiked teeth interlocking into bark near the tops of their trunks.

The sentries stood erect and resumed their posts.

Laney saw Allen—or a facsimile of her naked husband—interfacing with a saw palmetto. His fingers took on the same shade of green as he caressed the long, box cutter sharp blades. As usual, Allen seemed absorbed in his own little world.

Watching him, she couldn't help thinking back to the time when Allen had come home after showing the dermatologist the rash on his arm. The doctor hadn't seen any reason for concern, claiming the irritation would eventually go away.

But instead, the condition had only worsened, eventually taking over Allen's entire body: a metamorphosis beyond imagination; a terrifying transformation never experienced by any human being.

Even though Allen could assume the appearance of a human—most times only to appease Laney—it was only an illusion. His cellular makeup was no more human than a blade of grass, which basically is what he had become.

As he had long lost his appetite for human food, he fueled his body through photosynthesis basking in the sun thus producing chlorophylls accounting for his green skin tone.

After almost killing a man, they had fled the country to hide in the Amazon jungle where Allen soon discovered his true potential communing with the plant world, earning him the moniker—*The Botanist*—a name feared by the natives and those threatening the rainforest. It was there Allen and Laney had gone up against the logging division of Wilde Enterprises, sabotaging the operation, and putting themselves in the ruthless corporation's cross hairs.

Laney snapped out of it when she heard, "Hey there."

Allen walked slowly toward Laney between the raised plant beds. He held his hands out by his sides, his fingertips gracing each plant as he went along. As if to acknowledge their creator, every leaf bowed as if eager to be touched. The taller plants swooned, gracing his presence.

"Hey there, yourself," Laney replied.

Her husband strolled by his assortment of carnivorous pets: Venus flytraps large enough to entrap a small child, deep-throat pitcher plants, sticky sundews waiting to curl and ensnare a hapless prey.

Allen stopped to inspect his cure-all plants; each raceme blooming with scores of flowers ripe with pollen. He put out his jade-colored hand. A flower released its unique fruit. He rubbed his hand together, grinding the substance into a fine herb.

Laney grabbed a baggie from a box on the table, and held it open while Allen brushed his hands off, half-filling the pouch.

"I made you something." Allen picked up a hemp wristlet from the table.

"How sweet."

Allen slipped the bracelet onto her wrist. "Do you like it?"

"It's beautiful," she said, admiring the surprise gift. She felt a tickling sensation on her skin, not scratchiness, as though the charm was caressing her flesh. At first glance, it appeared a simple weave like a friendship bracelet a teenager might make. But when she examined the band closely, she saw the intricate detailed leafy patterns, so small it would take a magnifying glass to truly appreciate the craftsmanship.

"Promise me, you will never take it off."

Laney saw what she interpreted as a concerned look on Allen's face but couldn't be certain, as most times his features were a constant changing organism and often somewhat blurred.

"It's very important that you wear it at all times. As long as you have this on, no matter where you are, I'll be able to find you. That's how much I love you, Laney."

"And I love you, Allen Moss." Laney leaned forward and kissed her husband. She licked her lips. "You're sweet."

"I know."

"No, I mean you taste like citrus."

"Oh."

"Alice Kendrick stopped by."

"How is she doing?"

"Your cure-all did the trick. She's almost in remission."

"Glad to hear it." Allen formed what looked like a smile.

"I'm going to make myself some lunch. Come over to the cottage with me."

"What are you having?"

"I thought I'd make myself a salad."

"Really, Laney. A *salad*? No thank you. I think I'll stay here and hang out with my buds."

"Suit yourself."

* * *

Alice sat in the waiting room. She snatched a *Woman's Day* off the table. Five pages in, she realized it was the same issue she had browsed through during her previous visit and tossed it back down on the pile of outdated magazines.

She was tempted to leave but she had already checked in and thought it would be awkward if she just walked out of the office.

The door beside the check-in counter opened. A young woman in a floral scrub top stood in the doorway. "Alice Kendrick?"

"That's me." Alice scurried around the table and followed the medical assistant to a station where her blood pressure and temperature were taken. She was then brought to an examination room where she was asked to take a seat and assured the doctor would be in to see her shortly.

After ten minutes staring at the medical advice postings on the walls, the doctor entered the small room and sat in a chair across from her. "And how are we feeling today, Mrs. Kendrick?"

"Right as rain." She never understood why he always used the term "we" when it was she who was battling the disease, not him. She sat while he took his sweet time reviewing her file as though it was the first time he had ever seen her medical record.

If that wasn't enough, he had an annoying habit of clucking his tongue on the roof of his mouth while he read, which made her want to slap him silly.

He gazed up from the file and smiled. "Well, I have good news. The chemo seems to have done the trick. You, Alice Kendrick, are cancer free."

Alice returned the smile even though she knew he didn't deserve the credit for her miraculous recovery.

"Though I do have a question."

"What's that?" Alice asked.

"After reviewing the results of your latest blood panel, I noticed the lab had a problem concluding a portion of your tests."

"Oh?"

"Besides the chemo and the other medications I've prescribed, have you been taking any other drugs?"

"No. Does herbal tea count?"

"I doubt that would be it."

"Why do you ask?"

"Oh, it's not important. Well, enjoy the rest of your day."

Alice got up.

The doctor opened the door for her. She stepped out into the hall. He remained inside the room and closed the door.

Alice opened her purse, pretending to look for something. She could hear the doctor's voice. He was talking to someone on his cell phone. She heard bits and pieces and a name—Wilde Pharmaceuticals.

8

VISITOR

The prison guard at the gate waved Lucas through. He drove by the front of the main security building and pulled into his reserved parking spot. As the institution was privately owned and managed by Wilde Enterprises, Lucas was in charge of the operations under his title and overseeing the warden to some degree. The general population serving inside the walls of the Stoneham Correctional Facility was slightly over 2,000, the inmates' cells occupying two-thirds of the grounds, the other third set aside for other endeavors.

Lucas bypassed check-in stations using his high-level security cardkey as he made his way down corridors cleared of prisoners for his scheduled visit. He waited for a door with narrowly spaced steel bars to slide open. He stepped into an alcove, pushing the bar on the exit door to go outside. He crossed the small quad to another building.

Unlike the cellblock cordoned with passageways sectioning the correctional areas, the interior of the next building was spacious like an indoor basketball court. A twelve-foot high glass wall stretched across the room up to the ceiling. Lucas used his keycard to open the pneumatic door and entered the 10 million dollar science laboratory he had personally signed off on with the latest technology in genetic biology equipment so that the incarcerated Dr. Joel McCabe could continue his research uninterrupted.

His gray beard was shaggier since Lucas saw him last and the man's lab coat looked like he wore it to bed. McCabe sat at a workbench, peering through the lens of a digital microscope. He looked up at a flat-screen monitor on the tabletop of the blown-up microscope slide image. He heard Lucas approaching and turned on his stool. "So, Carter's little mouse is here to check up on me."

"Just my weekly visit." Lucas leaned against the workbench. When he took an interest in the globular mass displayed on the monitor, McCabe switched off the microscope and the screen went dark.

Lucas didn't give him the satisfaction by reacting. He was accustomed to the doctor's rudeness. He couldn't blame the man who was serving 3 consecutive life-term sentences for murder. As long as the brilliant geneticist kept providing results that was all that mattered. Lucas' job was to make sure McCabe had everything he needed so Lucas could relay reports back to Carter Wilde of the scientist's progress.

So far, his talents were beyond amazing. Not to mention frightening. There didn't seem to be a creature that McCabe couldn't conjure up like a witch's brew; the most astonishing part was that he no longer needed blood or tissue samples to create monsters like the ones from Cryptid Zoo.

He was creating his own artificial DNA replication models in the lab; hybrids never conceived possible in the molecular biology community.

"So what do you have to show me?" Lucas asked. Even though McCabe was difficult to work with and always kept his research close-lipped, he was still a bit of a showoff when it came to displaying his latest creation.

"You're going to love this," McCabe bragged. He led the way out of the laboratory to another part of the building leading up two flights of stairs. They came to a landing with a wide plate glass window overlooking three high-walled enclosures, each approximately one hundred feet square and at one time used as exercise yards for the inmates before Lucas converted the building for Dr. McCabe's research.

Large coils of triple concertina razor wire topped the thirty-foot tall walls on two of the enclosed areas.

McCabe picked up the receiver on a wall phone by the window. "It's feeding time."

Lucas looked down at the dual roll up doors in each enclosure. He watched as one began to rise. Two muscular men in prison uniforms, who looked like they spent every waking hour pumping iron, pushed a green dumpster out into the yard. The lid had been removed. Lucas could see food scraps inside the container most likely from the prison mess hall. The two men left the dumpster in the middle of the enclosure. They ran back inside the building and lowered the door.

The other door rose slowly.

A razorback boar the size of a water buffalo stormed out. It had massive tusks on its huge head. The giant pig must have smelled the discarded leftovers because it charged the 1-ton dumpster, smashing into the container head-on. Like a forklift, the powerful creature lifted the trash bin up with its tusks and toppled it onto its side, spilling the contents onto the ground. It lowered its head to root through the garbage.

"My god, McCabe. What the hell is that thing?"

"My latest cryptid. Behold, Hogzilla."

Lucas watched the hungry swine wade through the organic trash. He glanced over at the walled-in area without the barbwire. Large claw marks ran all the way up one of the walls. "I'm going to have to refortify that enclosure so don't be using it again. I can't believe you let those things get out."

"I underestimated them," McCabe said with a laugh. "I guess I made them too smart for their own good."

"And now, thanks to you, there's another liability running loose out there."

"So sue me," Dr. Joel McCabe snickered, knowing there wasn't much Lucas could do to him that he hadn't already done to himself; short of being locked away in solitary confinement on death row awaiting the needle.

But Lucas knew that was never going to happen. Carter Wilde had big plans for the bat shit crazy doctor.

On their way back down the stairs, McCabe took them on a different route. He leaned forward and swiped the cardkey hanging around his neck through the reader, opening a solid steel door.

Lucas had given the doctor the pass card, which only activated this particular entry so McCabe could direct the six prisoners that reported to him. The selected men were not allowed to associate with the other inmates in the facility.

As an enticement, they were awarded nicely furnished cells and three gourmet meals a day, Cuban cigars, and moderate amounts of top-notch bourbon whiskey, even the same brands Carter Wilde stocked in his personal wet bar up in his penthouse office suite. Lucas figured the more perks the men received, the less chance they would want to jeopardize their special treatment. Knowing what they knew, there was no going back into the general population for fear they might share their experiences working under the diabolical Dr. McCabe.

The one inmate that made the mistake of threatening to divulge what he'd seen was buried somewhere out in the nearby woods.

McCabe paused at an open doorway. He leaned against the doorjamb to watch the men inside the room sitting in front of a 60-inch big screen TV mounted on a wall plastered with centerpiece pinups of naked women ripped out of men's adult magazines.

The inmates ogled Jennie Lee on the screen, the famous traveling news reporter that made it her mission to cover stories relating to the Cryptid Zoo event. She was standing on an embankment, wearing a parka and a baseball cap with the news station's logo above the bill, holding a microphone. A man dressed in a dry-suit jacket stood by her side. Another man stood next to him, wearing a hunting hat and a camouflage coat with a shotgun cradled in the crook of his arm with the breech open.

Jenny Lee put the microphone up to her mouth. “With me are Don Favor and Miles Craver.” Jenny turned to Don Favor. “Mr. Favor, could you tell us what happened here today.” She held the microphone in front of his face.

“Well, I was kayaking in the slough when I was attacked.”

“Attacked? By what?”

“Some crazy bird. Big sucker too. It had this long beak and kept coming at me. I think it was trying to flip me out of the kayak.”

Jennie turned and faced the camera. “We have a short video that we have transferred on our feed taken by Mr. Craver on his cell phone who witnessed the attack.”

The screen was bordered on both sides by black matting of Don Favor in his kayak, waving his paddle at an enormous black bird with a twelve-foot wide wingspan hovering over the small watercraft, snapping its four-foot long red beak at the man.

The camera returned to Jennie Lee. “No, that wasn’t a pterosaur. What you just saw was a kongamato; another escapee from the infamous Cryptid Zoo.” She turned to the hunter. “So, Mr. Craver, were you able to shoot it?” Jennie extended her arm so the man could speak into the microphone.

“No, I was afraid of hitting Don.”

“Hey, you should have taken the shot,” Don said. “Damn things.”

“It took off on its own.”

Jennie turned to the camera. “And so, another incident. Thankfully, no one was hurt. This is Jennie Lee reporting. Back to you, Bill.”

The screen changed to an anchor team sitting behind the news desk.

An inmate with tattoos running up and down his arms switched the channel to a football game in progress.

Lucas looked at McCabe. The man had a big grin on his face.

The kongamatok was one of his.

9

NIGHT INTRUDER

Sophia raced out of the bathroom even before the toilet had stopped flushing. She scampered down the hall into her bedroom. She dove onto her bed and scrambled under her comforter with the Disney *Frozen* characters, Princess Anna and Elsa. Rosie was lying by the side of the bed in deep slumber. Her breathing had become more labored.

Miguel walked in and sat on the edge of the bed. "Brushed your teeth?"

Sophia opened her mouth wide to show off her sparkling white pearls.

He blocked his eyes with the back of his hand. "Whoa, don't blind me."

"You're being funny."

Miguel leaned down and kissed Sophia on the forehead. "Yeah, I am. You sleep tight."

"Did Mama tell you Tess's mom and us are going to see Coco?"

"The kids' movie?"

"Yeah, it's playing in town."

"Aren't you the busy bee, the movies, the big picnic this weekend." Miguel looked down at their fat Labrador snoring up a storm. "Don't forget to spend time with Rosie. I'm counting on you to look after her, especially when she has her pups."

"I will."

Miguel stood up from the bed and went to the door. He blew her a goodnight kiss like he did every bedtime. She snatched it out of the air and tucked it under her pillow. "Nighty night," he said, leaving the door open an inch to let in a sliver of light from the hall lamp.

He went in the other bedroom.

Maria was washing her face in the bathroom sink. "Will you and Bron be barbequing?"

"Yes, I signed us up as volunteers. There'll be plenty to do this picnic. Game booths, raffles, and rides for the kids; nothing too big though because of the tents but it should be fun. The forest service will be showing off their trucks and emergency vehicles. One of their rescue helicopters will be on display. I'm sure there'll be plenty of beer and wine to go around."

"I hope they have decent Merlot this time. Last year it was terrible."

"Two for one sale you get what you get."

Maria came in the room and sat on the edge of the bed. She reached over to her nightstand. She pushed the plunger down on a bottle of hand cream, squirting lotion onto her palm. She rubbed the moisturizer into her hands.

Miguel was about to take off his shirt when he heard a noise outside the window. He peered out the curtain but couldn't see anything in the dark.

"Miguel, what's wrong?"

"There's something prowling around out there." He started for the bedroom door.

"Where are you going?"

"To scare it off."

"Don't go out there."

There was a loud crash from the kitchen.

"Oh my God, Miguel. Sophia!"

"I'll get her."

"I'm going with you." Maria scurried over to the door next to her husband.

Miguel poked his head out the door. He'd left the light on over the kitchen sink.

A shadow cast across the kitchen floor. Judging by the shape of the silhouette moving on the far wall, the animal was big and stood on two legs. He could hear raspy breathing. The beast brushed against the kitchen table, causing the bottom of the legs to screech. Plates and glasses smashed to the floor. A large appliance crashed down.

Miguel turned to Maria. "When I switch off our bedroom light, make a mad dash for Sophia's room. I'll kill the hall light as we go. Ready?"

Maria nodded.

"Go." Miguel turned off the wall switch and the room went dark. He skirted out the door. Maria was right behind him. They tried to be as quiet as possible. Reaching Sophia's door, Maria slipped in first while Miguel reached across to the other wall to turn off the hall light.

He heard a guttural snarl and glanced down the hall toward the kitchen. The animal stood at the edge of the light. From what he could see, the thing was enormous.

The creature watched Miguel; its growl a deep-throated rumbling.

Miguel flicked off the light and ducked into Sophia's room. He shut the door, locking it. Miguel knew the flimsy bedroom door wasn't going to keep the thing out for long and looked around. He spotted Sophia's dresser with a vanity mirror. It didn't weigh much but it might serve as a temporary barrier. He got around to the side of the dresser and shoved it in front of the door.

Maria was sitting on the bed with her hand over Sophia's mouth, shushing their daughter. "You have to be quiet."

Sophia's eyes grew wide with fright.

"It's okay," Miguel assured her.

Rosie woke up. She sat by the foot of Sophia's bed. Her hackles stood up like short, black porcupine spines; her gaze fixed on the bedroom door.

A thunderous bang knocked down a picture of Sophia and Rosie posing on the back porch. The wooden frame broke apart and glass shattered as it hit the hardwood floor.

Sophia screamed.

The beast roared on the other side of the door.

"My God, Miguel, what is that thing?"

"It's a bigfoot."

The creature threw its body up against the bedroom door, splitting it down the middle.

"Both of you, off the bed." Miguel waited for Maria to pick Sophia up. He grabbed the edge of the box spring frame and dragged the bed halfway in front of the dresser to further fortify the door. He put his hip against the dresser.

Another heavy thud struck the door. The vanity mirror cracked and triangular shaped pieces of glass fell onto the dresser top. The fissure down the center of the door widened even more.

Rosie went berserk, barking.

The door bowed inward. A malevolent eye peered through the crack.

Miguel picked up a jagged piece of broken mirror. He shoved it at the peephole.

The creature roared with fury when the jagged glass drove deep into its eye. It lurched away from the door, slamming into the wall, and stomped down the hall.

"Rosie, quiet," Miguel said. It was impossible to hear anything with her loud barking echoing in the room. He put his hand on her neck, rubbing her fur to calm her down. "Good girl."

"What do we do?" Maria asked, her arms around Sophia.

"I guess we wait. Make sure it's gone." Miguel knelt next to Rosie, the two keeping a vigilant watch on the door while Maria and Sophia huddled together.

* * *

The rooftop emergency strobe lights on the sheriff's cruiser lit up the side of the house in a brilliant gala of flickering reds and blues.

Inside, Maria worked to clean up the mess in the kitchen while Miguel gave their statement to Sheriff Abraham "Abe" Stone.

"You're lucky no one was hurt," Abe said, glancing about the kitchen. The china hutch looked like it had fallen off the back of a fast-moving truck, glassware and dishes smashed everywhere, a couple of broken chairs. The refrigerator toppled over with the door hanging open; food spilt out. Large footprints mashed on the leftovers leaving a trail out the doorway, the kitchen door kindling lying on the floor.

"This is the set my mom gave us," Maria grumbled, scooping up shards of dishes in a dustpan.

"So, could it have been a bear?" Abe asked, ready to make a note in his small spiral pad.

"No, it was a bigfoot."

"Sure it wasn't a big cat? There've been sightings and I've been getting complaints about missing livestock."

"Believe me, I know a bigfoot when I see it."

Abe stuffed his notepad in his shirt pocket. "Let me help you right your fridge." He used his boot to move the plastic drawer and mushy milk cartons out of the way. Abe and Miguel stood the refrigerator up and pushed it back against the wall. Maria tossed ruined food items in a trash bin.

"Better keep the shotgun handy," Abe advised. "Need any help buttoning up that door?"

"I have a sheet of plywood in the shed."

"Let's get to it then." Abe stepped outside. He went over to the cruiser, leaned in through the open window, and switched off the emergency lights.

The woods around the house went pitch dark.

Abe watched Miguel walk across the yard and open the shed. Miguel pulled down the drawstring, turning on the light bulb hanging on the ceiling rafter. He came out wearing a tool belt and hefting a 4 by 8 foot sheet of plywood.

Once the covering was in place, Abe held it firmly over the doorjamb while Miguel fastened the plywood to the wall with his battery-operated screwdriver.

"Thanks for your help," Miguel said, shaking Abe's hand.

"Anytime. You folks take care. Any more trouble, give me a call."

"Will do, Abe. Night."

"Night now." Abe got inside the cruiser. He started the engine and backed away from the house, turning on his headlights.

He headed out on the rural road, passing the Banner house. After traveling five miles he turned down the long gravel driveway to his home; a farmhouse with a barn and a large pen of grazing goats, a business his wife, Clare, ran manicuring the neighbors' grasslands.

As he pulled up to the front porch, he could see the light was still on meaning Clare had waited up for him. He stopped and shut off the engine. Climbing out of the car, he could hear the goats moving about in their pens.

Abe went up the porch steps, making sure to stomp his boots on the front mat before going inside.

Clare sat by the fire, reading a Linwood Barclay novel. Rounder was curled up in front of the hearth next to her chair. Abe's wife of thirty years looked over her shoulder as he came into the living room. "You're out late."

"Miguel says a bigfoot broke into their house." Abe unbuckled his gun belt and laid it on the fold-down leaf of the writing desk.

"My lord, are they okay?" Clare placed her bookmark on the page and closed the book.

"Their place got busted up but no one was hurt." Abe slumped in his recliner. He bent over, undid his shoelaces, and took off his boots. He stretched his legs out so he could feel the warmth of the fire on the bottoms of his stockinged feet.

He looked over at the mammoth dog slumbering by the fire. "Rounder have the night off?"

Normally, Rounder would be inside his sentry shelter next to the pens watching over the goats. Lately, Clare had been pampering him, letting him spend more time indoors. She'd raised him from a pup, keeping him in constant contact with the goats to become a Livestock Guardian Dog. The Great Pyrenees Mountain Dog weighed almost 130 pounds. He was a massive canine with long, thick, white hair and a bushy mane common for the French breed, which protected the animal's throat against large predators like wolves.

"I just finished brushing him out and cleaning his ears. Thought it might do him good to spend some time beside the fire."

"No pedicure?"

"That's tomorrow." As Rounder spent a large part of his day chasing after the goats on the rough ground, it was important to keep his nails trimmed and to routinely check the pads on his paws for possible injuries that might cause him to go lame.

Clare got up from her chair. "I better tuck him in so we can go to bed."

"I can do that." Abe reached for his boots.

"No, you sit."

"Yes, Master."

Clare slapped the side of her leg and headed toward the kitchen.

"That's your cue," Abe said.

Rounder kept his chin on his paws. Though he was loyal and protective, he could be stubborn and slow to obey whenever it suited him. The one thing that always got his attention was a stern command from Clare.

"Rounder, come!"

The headstrong dog lifted its head abruptly.

It pained Abe to see Rounder struggle to get up. The large breed dog was starting to show early signs of hip dysplasia. But once he was up on all fours, he trampled off into the kitchen like a champion, following Clare out the backdoor.

Abe took a moment to decompress and stared at the fireplace, watching the flames dance in the hearth like writhing red snakes. As much as he tried to clear his mind, he couldn't help worrying about that creature Miguel had described and if Rounder—as fierce and gallant as he was—would have a fighting chance if it came for the goats.

10

THE RAID

Jack had just fallen asleep when he was jolted awake by two loud thumps on the outside wall of the cabin. He immediately shook Nora. "Wake up," he whispered.

"Huh?" Nora responded groggily.

"Lennie just gave the signal."

Jack threw back the covers and slipped off the bed onto the floor. He was wearing a T-shirt, briefs, and socks as the interior of the cabin was warm and toasty from the heat generated from the wood-burning stove.

Nora got off the bed. She stayed low, crawling on her hands and knees.

Jack pushed the rug back covering the trapdoor. He grabbed the recessed ring and raised the hatch. He held the lid so Nora could scoot down the steps leading to the root cellar. He was about to follow her when he spotted a thin red line stab through the glass of the window, tracking a red dot on the opposite wall. Two more sharpshooters' infrared laser beams shone through the windowpane to conduct their own search for a target.

Suddenly, a bright spotlight lit up the room. A merciless barrage of gunfire ripped through the walls, blowing out the windows. High-velocity slugs pelted every square inch, demolishing furniture and shredding everything into exploding unrecognizable pieces. Jack could hear the rapid fire of the gun suppressors, like a carpenter crew was outside shooting nail guns at the cabin.

Jack dropped the lid and scurried down the steps. Nora was already dressed in jeans, a flannel shirt, and boots having prepared for this very moment. Jack grabbed a set of clothes hanging on a hook and put them on. He shoved his stockinged feet into a pair of slip-on boots so as not to waste time with laces. They threw on their coats and grabbed already packed duffle bags filled with clothes and supplies.

Holding up a battery-operated lamp, Jack led the way down the underground passage. He heard a muffled bang above as the front door was kicked in. He knew it would only be a matter of seconds before they discovered the trapdoor under all the debris.

Jack and Nora scurried down the narrow tunnel, crouching most of the way. Jack heard the distinct sound of the trapdoor slamming onto the cabin floor and heavy footsteps coming down the stairs.

A set of crude steps was farther down at the end of the dirt corridor.

Jack turned off the lamp. He went up the steps, pushing aside a flat layer of brush concealing the tunnel entrance. He tossed out his bag and climbed out of the hole. Nora threw her duffle up. He dropped it on the ground and helped her out.

Jack could hear approaching boots charging through the subterranean passage.

A commando wearing a tactical helmet with night vision goggles climbed halfway through the hole and gazed up. He froze suddenly when he saw the yeren towering over him, holding a large boulder above his head. The man ducked into the tunnel just as Lennie released the two hundred pound rock, which crashed down, sealing the hole in the ground.

"Come on. That bought us a little time." They grabbed the bags and ran. Jack knew the commandos wouldn't waste time trying to move the heavy boulder and would have to double back underground to the cabin. He had no idea how many there were, only that they had no intention of taking him or Nora alive. That was quite evident after the destruction to the cabin. He wasn't sure if their intentions were to capture the yeren alive or hunt it down and kill it. Either way, it wouldn't be good for Lennie.

Slivers of moonlight etched through the treetops. Jack and Nora ran blindly down the forest path without fear of crashing into a tree trunk or stumbling and falling at a sudden bend in the trail. They had practiced this escape route hundreds of times—even blindfolded—to ensure a quick getaway without relying on flashlights their pursuers would easily spot in the woods.

They ran for fifteen minutes, zigzagging onto side trails to cover their tracks before stopping at an embankment of loose rock overlooking a desolate dirt road. A high barrier of shrubbery skirted the tree line on the opposite shoulder.

Jack was about to head down the hill when Nora grabbed him by the arm. "Jack, there's someone down there."

As he lowered to a crouch, Jack saw a figure step out of the bushes. The military-clad commando stood in the middle of the dirt road. He was carrying an AA-12 Atchisson fully automatic 12-gauge shotgun with a 32 round drum magazine.

Jack had seen such a weapon in action and what it could do to a human body.

The commando looked down the road to his left then stared the other way. He glanced up the hillock.

Afraid she was visible from below, Nora ducked farther behind a tree. Her boot slipped out from under her, kicking away a stone. The rock caused more stones to dislodge and tumble down the steep slope. The commando raised his weapon and opened fire.

A fast succession of shotgun blasts belched a torrent of pellets, pulverizing the bark off the trees and sending a rain of leaves down on Jack and Nora's heads.

Jack undid the zipper on his duffle bag. He rummaged around the clothes and survival supplies for his revolver.

Then came a dead silence.

Jack peeked out from behind the tree trunk. The commando had dropped his spent magazine on the ground. He took a smaller 8 round clip from his ammo belt. He slapped it into the bottom of the shotgun, drawing back the slide to put the next cartridge into the chamber. He started up the rocky hillside.

Jack kept digging around for his gun. Then it dawned on him that he had been sifting through Nora's bag. In their haste to get away from the tunnel, he had grabbed her bag by mistake. He looked over at Nora, pointing at the duffle by her knee. "That's my bag. Get my gun." He could hear the man's boots crunching up the rock.

Nora unzipped the bag. She felt around inside searching for Jack's handgun.

Jack braced himself. The commando was only ten feet away. One shot from the lethal firearm would be enough to blow off an arm. He was so close Jack could hear the man's labored breathing.

Nora pulled out Jack's gun. She was about to toss him the weapon when the commando stepped between the trees and aimed...

Lennie snatched the shotgun's hot barrel, ripped it from the commando's hands, and tossed it away. The man gaped at the twelve-foot tall yeren then reached for his sidearm. He screamed when Lennie wrenched his arm back in an unnatural position and bone snapped. As if annoyed by the man's bellowing, Lennie picked him up and heaved him twenty feet into the trees.

"That was subtle," Jack said to the big ape-man. Lennie grunted like it was no big deal. He turned to Nora to make sure she was okay. When she smiled up at him, the lummox started down the hill.

Jack and Nora grabbed their bags and followed Lennie.

When they got down to the road, Jack rushed into the bushes. He cleared a path to the large white moving van mostly concealed under camouflage netting. He yanked the cover off onto the ground then opened the rollup door. Stacks of feedbags and a row of 5-gallon water jugs were flushed up against the front wall of the 28-foot long cargo hold. The floor was covered with leaves, peat moss, and hay.

"Hurry it up, big guy. We're going for a ride." Jack grabbed an ear of corn from a crate by the door to coax the yeren over. It worked like a charm. Lennie lumbered over and grabbed the corn out of Jack's hand, crunching it up with one bite. Jack took out some more maize and tossed them into the truck bed. Lennie stepped up on the back bumper. He ducked his head to clear the 9-foot tall ceiling and sat down on the blanket of leaves. The rear suspension sagged under his weight.

"Move up a little." Jack climbed up and gave Lennie a nudge on the shoulder. The yeren scooted to the middle of the truck bed. Jack made sure the skylight on the roof was cracked open to allow airflow inside the cargo container. He grabbed the strap attached to the bottom of the rollup door and jumped down to the ground, pulling the door down with him.

Jack ran up to the driver's side and climbed up into the cab.

Nora was already sitting in the passenger seat. "Is he settled in?"

"For now." Jack knew Lennie could be unpredictable whenever he was kept in a confined space for too long. There was no telling how long they would have to be on the road. Maybe the ride would lull the yeren into a peaceful sleep; wouldn't that be wonderful.

Jack turned the ignition key and fired up the diesel engine. He slipped the transmission into gear, stomping on the accelerator.

The moving van burst through the bushes, turned, and barreled off down the forest service road into the night.

* * *

After combing the cabin and finding nothing, Ivan Connors ordered his men to fan out and search the forest. It took nearly half an hour before he got a call on his radio that one of his men had been found and was severely injured.

By the time Connors arrived, the man had been given morphine for the pain but he was still having screaming fits. Looking at the man's contorted arm, Connors couldn't really blame him though the noise was getting on Connors' nerves. "Who did this to you?"

The man grimaced, eyes clinched shut as he battled the pain. "Damn thing threw me into the trees."

"What about Tremens and the professor? Did you see them?"

"Yeah. Then that creature jumped me."

"Did you see which way they went?" Connors asked.

"No." The man opened his eyes and looked up at Connors. His face was more lucid. The morphine had kicked in. "I found their truck."

"Truck, what truck?"

"A white moving van."

Connors looked at the other dozen or so men standing around him. They shook their heads. "Damn it to hell. We'll never find them."

The man with the grotesquely twisted arm gave Connors a drug-induced grin. "I put a GPS tracker under their wheel well."

11

THE CINEMA

Denny Jameson spent a few minutes posting the new screen times on the Rocklin Falls Cinema website, one of his many duties as manager of the movie theater and supervisor of his small staff of four.

Ernie worked the projectionist booth, operating the old-style two-reel system, the theater's meager budget unable to upgrade to a high-definition digital video projector used in the strip mall Cineplexes. Gary, cashier in the ticket booth. Tina and Louie ran the concession stand. Louie was also usher and gathered up the trash left in the theater after each performance.

The owner had been on Denny's case to organize his desk and clean up his office, as it was becoming a mini-warehouse. Unable to find the key that unlocked the rear door to the receiving area—suspecting an employee had lost it or taken it home—Denny had been allowing the deliveryman to bring shipments in through the front lobby and park the boxes in his office on the first floor.

Food and drink items were kept in a room behind the concession stand while cleaning supplies were taken upstairs to be stored in the janitor's supply room.

Denny glared at the four cardboard boxes filled with plastic bottles of liquid carpet and upholstery cleaner. As many patrons had left notes in the *How Can We Improve Our Theater* suggestion box, complaining the floors in the theaters were sticky and the seats were stained from spilled drinks and ground-in buttered popcorn, Denny's boss decided it was high-time the theater had a major clean-up. Being the cheapskate that he was, he decided not to call in a professional cleaning crew and assigned the task to Denny and his minions.

Normally, Denny would have told Gary or Louie to take the boxes upstairs but they were too busy with the large crowds of chaperoned kids for the Saturday matinee of the animated-fantasy *Coco*. He figured they would need the cleaning supplies from two boxes, which meant he would have to carry the other two cases upstairs to the janitor's closet.

It was going to be a long day and the first performance hadn't even started. Denny had scheduled the last showing to end at five o'clock in the afternoon so they could start the monumental task of cleaning the theater. He figured if they tackled it together, they could be done in three or four hours. He hoped he didn't have to listen to their griping about being too tired from working a grueling shift and then being expected to work overtime scrubbing and cleaning.

Denny got up from his desk. He went over to the door and scooted a box across the carpet to prop it open. He could hear the kids' excited voices as they funneled into the lobby and lined up at the concession stand.

Afraid someone might enter his office if he left the door open, he picked up a box—damn thing had to weigh forty pounds—and put it on the floor just outside his door. He pushed the box holding the door open back inside his office so the door would close.

He bent down and picked up the box, making sure to bend his knees so as not to strain his back. Holding the box by the bottom, he could just see over the top. The stairs were at the end of the corridor. He could hear the kids stampeding behind him, hustling into the theater.

Reaching the bottom of the stairs, he looked up at the ten steps. As he couldn't see his feet, he had to be especially careful going up and take it slowly so as not to trip and fall. The last thing he needed was to get injured and not be able to tackle the big project.

He felt around with his right foot and found the first step. He lifted his left foot onto the same step then raised his right foot to the next step. He repeated the process; halfway up he nearly lost his balance and thought he might fall backwards but he regained his forward momentum and kept going.

Once on the landing, he dropped the box on the floor. His shoulders and arms ached. He dreaded the thought of having to make another trip.

He walked over to a door with a placard: STAFF ONLY.

He opened the door. Ernie was placing a large reel on the projector.

Denny didn't want to distract the projectionist so he walked away without saying a word, leaving the door open.

He picked up the box and carried it to the end of the landing to a door labeled JANITOR SUPPLIES. He put the box on the floor.

He reached in his pocket and pulled out a small key chain. He slipped the key marked JS into the lock. He pushed open the door then picked up the box, stepping inside the supply room. It was the size of a small bedroom with metal shelves along three walls stocked with various janitorial cleaning products.

Denny could feel a cold breeze coming down on his head. He tripped on some clutter on the floor and dropped the box. The floor was littered with smashed ceiling tiles and chunks of wood.

He looked up and saw the morning sky through the ten-foot round gaping hole in the roof. He heard a strange sound like leather tarps rustling together.

Six massive creatures stared down at him from atop the metal shelves. They looked like black Great Danes with folded wings, sitting on their haunches.

The megabats swooped down before Denny could open his mouth to scream.

12

RAISINETTES

Betsy Banner and her daughter, Tess, stood with Sophia while Maria purchased the movie tickets from Gary sitting in the booth. They came to the Rocklin Falls Cinema so often they knew all the employees by name as it was a small town. They followed Maria into the lobby where Tina was waiting. Maria handed her the tickets. She ripped off the stubs and handed the tickets back to Maria.

"Thank you, Maria," Betsy said. "You sure it wasn't my turn?"

"You got *Beauty and the Beast* last time, remember," Maria reminded her friend. Every time a children's movie was released, Maria and Betsy would take turns paying whenever they brought their daughters.

Sophia and Tess ran up to the concession stand to check out the candy selection in the glass counter.

"Thank you for suggesting we see *Coco*," Betsy said. "I don't know if I could sit through another one of those *Despicable Me*."

"Actually, it was Sophia's choice."

Betsy laughed. "Wasn't that a Meryl Streep movie?"

"I think that was *Sophie's Choice*."

"You don't think *Coco* will be too scary for the girls?"

"What do you mean?"

"Isn't it about the Day of the Dead?"

"Yes. Dia de Muertos, the Mexican holiday. Day of the Dead is somewhat like Halloween. It's a time to honor the dead."

"So it's not a zombie movie?"

"No, Betsy," Maria smiled. "Rest assured. It's not a George Romero zombie movie."

"Mama, can Tess and I get drinks and share a big popcorn?" Sophia asked Maria.

"Sure. Just as long as you don't smother it with too much butter at the pump. That's a new outfit."

"It's okay, Mrs. Walla. We'll get plenty of napkins," Tess piped in.

Maria looked at Betsy. "Would you like anything?"

"No, I'm okay." Betsy leaned in and whispered, "I brought us a couple of bottled waters and our own snacks." She lifted the strap on her shoulder to show off her bulging bag of goodies.

"You're going to put this place out of business," Maria smirked. "Don't you know they make their money at the concession stand and not ticket sales?"

"I brought your favorites."

"Don't tell me...Raisinettes?"

"That's not all. I also brought some candy bars: Look, Abba-Zaba, Big Hunk—"

"Egad. Last time I had one of those I lost a filling."

Once the girls had their large popcorn—and drenched it with butter against Maria's wishes—they went through the doorway into the auditorium to grab their seats.

A single aisle extended down to the front between twenty rows of seats with ten chairs in each row on each side.

Many seats were already occupied with restless kids and bored parents staring at the brightly lit screens on their cell phones.

"I refuse to sit in the front row," Betsy said as they made their way down the center aisle. "Last time I did that, my neck ached for a week."

Maria glanced to her left and right. "Look for some seats together."

"There're four." Betsy hurried to the right side. She stood at the end of a row and pointed to the vacant seats on the other side of an elderly couple. Betsy turned and whispered to Maria, "Oh shoot, it's Bernie and Becky Bickerson."

Maria recognized the two right away though she forgot their real names. They were a running joke around town because wherever the annoying couple went they were always quarreling about the silliest things. As much as Maria loved living in a tightly knit community, the small town gossip could be a little cruel, especially when someone was branded with a nickname. She remembered Miguel telling her about a promiscuous gal who hung out at the roadside bar some of the guys called Fonda Peters.

In order to get to the seat, Becky and Bernie had to stand and flip their seats up so Sophia and Tess could pass, followed by Betsy and then Maria.

"Sorry," Maria apologized to Bernie as she squeezed between his fat belly and the seatback.

"Don't expect us to be getting up every time you need to run to the bathroom."

Bernie's wife gave him a look. "Says you, Mister Weak Prostrate."

"Hey, I don't need you telling everyone my business."

"Pipe down, you old coot."

"Who you calling an old coot?"

"Just sit on the aisle and hush."

"Fine, if it will shut you up." Bernie switched places with his wife.

Maria sat down next to Betsy, a seat away from the Bickersons.

"That was fun," Betsy whispered in Maria's ear.

"Which is why I prefer renting movies and watching them at home."

"Yes, but would you have these?" Betsy opened the bag on her lap. She put her cell phone inside and turned on the faceplate. "Take your pick."

Maria reached in and took out an Abba-Zaba. She bent the candy bar back and forth to soften it up. Then she ripped the wrapping paper and put a piece of candy in her mouth. She had to grip the white taffy between her teeth and bite down hard to get through to the peanut butter center. Once she had bitten off a portion it was best to just let the taffy dissolve slowly in her mouth and not be tempted to chew if she didn't want to end up visiting the dentist.

Betsy held up her cell phone. "Better shut 'em off."

Maria reached in her pocket. She took out her phone, and held the button down until the screen went blank.

The overhead lights dimmed for the preview attractions. Maria settled back in her chair. A dramatic score and revving engines blared over the surround-sound speakers as a fast cutting car chase action sequence flashed on the big screen. Maria hoped the loud noise and the blink-of-an-eye editing didn't give her a headache.

Another movie trailer had just started when Maria heard, "Tess, look what you made me do."

Maria leaned forward and looked over at the girls. The front of Sophia's sweatshirt and jeans were covered with greasy popcorn. To top it off, she had spilled her drink on her lap.

Tess righted the knocked-over bucket. "Sorry, Sophia."

"Let's go to the restroom and get you cleaned up." Maria stood. She motioned for Sophia to follow her.

The Bickersons were too engrossed watching Dwayne "The Rock" Johnson pummeling a couple of soldiers to notice Maria patiently waiting for them to move their feet so they could get by.

"Excuse us."

Bernie looked up and frowned at Maria.

At first, she didn't think he was going to budge. "Can we get by?" she asked, having to raise her voice so as to be heard over the loud soundtrack.

"Movie hasn't even started and you're already up and down." He got up to stand in the aisle. "Come on, don't take all day."

The elderly woman drew her feet under her chair so Maria and Sophia could pass. Maria ignored the old grouch. She waited for Sophia and they walked up the aisle.

"I'm sorry, Mama," Sophia said as they stepped into the lobby and the door closed behind them.

"It's all right." Maria was glad to be out of the loud theater. She hoped the main feature wasn't as noisy. She could feel the building pressure of a headache coming on.

She took a moment to inspect the front of Sophia's clothes. The buttered popcorn had left greasy stains on Sophia's sweatshirt; more blotches were on the thighs of her pants from the spilt drink. There was a chance some cold water might prevent the outfit from becoming a total loss.

Sophia's eyes widened. "Mama, what's that?"

Maria turned. She saw something black gliding down the corridor. She grabbed Sophia and pulled her down on the floor next to the wall.

The giant bat swooped into the lobby and crashed down on the concession counter, smashing the glass top with its talon feet. Tina was standing by the popcorn machine and screamed. Flapping its wings, the bat lunged at the young woman.

Louie bolted out from a backroom. He took one look at the vicious creature attacking his co-worker and grabbed a broom. He thrust the end into the bat. The bat screeched.

Maria hugged Sophia as two more giant bats swooped down the stairs from the second floor. Their wingspans had to be at least ten feet across. She remembered Miguel telling her about huge megabats called ahools that had escaped from Cryptid Zoo and were never found.

And here they were, of all places, in a movie theater packed with children.

Maria covered Sophia's eyes when an ahool landed on Louie's back and savagely tore off the side of his face.

"We can't stay here," Maria whispered to Sophia. They stayed low and skirted along the wall. Maria led the way down the short entrance into the men's restroom and ducked around the corner. She wished there was a proper door she could barricade. She glanced around at the sinks, the metal privacy screen at one end of a row of urinals, the six toilet stall doors, looking for the best place to hide.

"Mama!"

Maria heard a bat fly into the restroom's alcove. "Hurry, in here." Maria pulled Sophia into a toilet stall and closed the door. She turned the lock.

The giant bat swooped in and landed, its sharp-clawed feet clicking on the ceramic tile floor. The creature let out a bellowing *HOOOOH!*

Maria looked at Sophia and put her finger up to her lips. She motioned for Sophia to stand on the toilet seat.

Sophia shook her head.

Maria gave her a stern look.

The girl held her nose and pointed into the bowl.

The last person to use the toilet had neglected to flush properly. A disposable toilet seat cover was floating on top of brown water.

Maria leaned down and peeked under the stall door. She could see the five-foot tall bat walking clumsily about the floor like a hunched drunkard in a black cape.

The bat must have heard her because it turned its head and hissed.

"Get up, NOW!" Maria snapped at her daughter.

Sophia grabbed the toilet paper dispenser to steady herself and stepped up onto the toilet seat. She refused to look down, sitting back on the stainless steel flushing mechanism.

A door banged open a few stalls away.

Sophia let out a whimper.

Maria turned and put her finger back up to her lips.

Her daughter pressed her back against the wall. She slipped and her hand came down on the flusher handle.

The toilet made a gurgling sound.

"No, no," Maria groaned, watching the brown water rise in the bowl.

The ahool screeched and rammed its body against the stall door.

* * *

Betsy gazed over her shoulder expecting to see Maria and Sophia coming back down the aisle. She couldn't imagine what was taking them so long. The movie had already begun. She knew Sophia would be disappointed missing the beginning. Tess was eating the last of the popcorn left in the bucket. As Tess had spilled the popcorn, Betsy knew she would have to be the one to make another run to the concession stand if she didn't want the two girls to get into a squabble.

Where were they?

The animated characters on the big screen suddenly went herky-jerky, the movie frames flickering like the film had jumped off the sprocket.

Betsy looked up at the projectionist window. The reel had stopped but the lamp was still shining white light on the screen. The theater became quiet as the surround-sound speakers went mute.

Bernie jumped out of his seat. He turned and yelled up at the small porthole window in the projection booth, “Hey, up there! Wake up!”

He was answered by a high-pitched scream.

“Mom, who was that?” Tess dropped the bucket of popcorn on the seat beside her.

“We need to leave.” Betsy glanced at the red exit sign over the door in the front of the auditorium.

“But we haven’t seen the movie.”

“I know but something’s not right.”

“Where’re Sophia and her mom?”

“I’m not sure. Let’s go to the lobby and find them.”

Half a dozen adults were standing with puzzled looks on their faces. A few frightened children were whining for their mothers.

Betsy heard a loud crash from overhead. Acoustic tiles fell from the ceiling, landing on parents and evoking screams from the children.

An enormous creature swooped out from a hole in the ceiling. It soared over the rows of seats, hovering above the front stage, the projector beam casting its silhouette on the big screen.

The image looked like a monstrous flying dragon.

“Who the hell let that thing in?” Bernie yelled.

Another creature dove into the theater creating a pandemonium of screams as everyone scrambled down the narrow rows for the main aisle.

Betsy pulled Tess down between the seats. She whispered to the elderly lady in the next seat. “Ma’am, get down with us.”

The woman was too distracted reaching across the vacant seat, trying to get her husband’s attention.

A creature landed across the aisle—a giant bat.

Perched on the seatback, it had to be five feet tall. Betsy could feel the draft when it opened its massive wings to balance itself. It had a grotesque fox-like face with savage teeth and pointy ears.

Bernie stood in the aisle, frozen with fear.

The bat glared at Bernie and bared its sharp fangs.

Bernie was too terrified to notice the other bat swooping down on him. It snatched Bernie up by the shoulders with its curled talons, dragging him to the front of the theater.

The creature across the aisle, leaped on the woman. It wrapped its wings around her like Dracula covering his victim with his cape to take a bite out of her neck, muffling her scream as it fed. She kicked her feet against the seatback for a few brief seconds, then stopped.

Unable to get to the aisle, Betsy took Tess by the hand and they climbed over the seats in front of them. They had made it down only two rows when the giant bat that had abducted Bernie, ascended on the first row of seats, blocking their path.

Betsy could see the man lying motionless on the floor by the stage. She knelt on the floor. She rummaged through her purse for her cell phone. Each time she thought she found it, it was a stupid candy bar.

"Damn it, come on." She kept searching for her phone.

Tess started crying.

The bats soared back and forth in the theater.

Betsy had never heard so many people screaming at one time.

13

FEATURE MATINEE

Miguel and Bron worked with the many volunteers getting the fairground on the edge of town ready for the Rocklin Falls Grand Picnic. They weren't expecting the same turnout as the previous year, which had been over a thousand people. This year, attendance was expected to be half that if they were lucky. Many residents in the neighboring rural communities had safety concerns about the outdoor event and chose not to participate.

But there were those that refused to live in fear. In Miguel's opinion, being attacked by a cryptid was no different than any other wild animal though precautions had been put in place, which was why the entire fairground was now completely surrounded with a twelve-foot tall security fence.

A permanent picnic area cover with a pitched corrugated panel roof stood over a slab of concrete large enough to accommodate fifty picnic tables and benches, a brick barbeque with ten separate cooking grates, and a long serving counter.

Miguel, Bron, and a team of men were finishing with the last massive canopy tent of the six they had erected to shelter the game booths, exhibits, and stands used by locals selling their homemade goods.

"Where do you want this one?" a voice called out.

Miguel saw Dave McElroy standing on the raised platform of a rental cherry picker. "Park it over there." Miguel pointed to a far corner of the chain link fence. "That'll give us complete coverage of the entire fairground."

"Sure thing." Dave operated the controls and drove slowly away.

As a precaution, the picnic organizers had insisted the event have added security with lookout posts. Instead of building permanent structures on all four corners, it was decided cherry pickers would be a more economical solution with an experienced hunter posted on each boom lift.

Miguel was watching Bron loop a tie-down around a stake when Miguel's phone chimed in his pocket. He took it out and stared at the screen. He put the phone up to his ear. "Hello? What? I can't understand you. Is that Sophia screaming?"

Bron looked up. "Miguel, something wrong?"

"We're on our way." Miguel shoved the phone in his pocket. He glanced at Bron. "That was Maria. There's trouble at the theater."

The men bolted for Miguel's truck.

Racing out of the fairground, it took only five minutes to reach the Rocklin Falls Cinema. Sheriff Stone's cruiser was parked askew at the curb; the driver's door left standing open. Miguel pulled up right behind and shut off the engine.

Shots rang out inside the theater.

Miguel and Bron jumped from the truck and rushed to the front entrance. The door swung open. A terrified woman carrying a hysterical girl ran out. More adults and frightened children scrambled out, fleeing the theater.

Miguel wanted to stop someone and ask what was going on but he could tell everyone was too scared as they ran out onto the sidewalk and into the street.

Once the path was clear, Miguel and Bron stormed into the lobby.

Sheriff Stone stood by the concession stand counter. He leveled his gun on a huge creature withering on the floor and fired a single shot into its head. He looked over at Miguel and Bron as they approached. "Counting this one, I've killed two."

Miguel glanced around and saw another giant bat sprawled on the carpet. Two employees wearing matching red polo shirts were lying dead amongst the pooling blood and shattered glass.

"How many are there?" Miguel asked.

"Not sure. I think there might be more inside the theater."

Sheriff Stone and Bron followed Miguel over to the door. They peeked inside the auditorium. Two megabats flew about the large space, staying close to the white screen lit up by the beam of light from the projection booth.

Miguel could see the tops of heads hunkered down between the seats.

"Jesus, Miguel. Do you think Betsy, Maria, and the girls are in there?"

"I didn't see them run out." Miguel turned to Bron. "We need to get up there and shut down the projector."

"Why's that?" Sheriff Stone asked.

“Ahools aren’t like regular bats. As they’re so big they’ve lost their echolocation abilities. Kill the light and they won’t be able to navigate in the dark.”

“In other words, they’ll be grounded.”

“And easier to kill.”

“I’ll go.” Bron ran off down the corridor toward the stairs.

Miguel heard a child screaming behind him. He turned to see who it was. The cry was coming from the men’s restroom. It sounded like Sophia.

Sheriff Stone heard it, too.

As soon as they rushed into the public lavatory, Miguel got a whiff of backed-up plumbing and saw the floor flooded with foul water.

A giant bat was standing on the lip of a toilet stall door. It pulled in its wings, ready to jump down into the partition.

Miguel was afraid a bullet might ricochet into the stall so he motioned to the sheriff not to use his gun. They snuck up on the megabat. Miguel grabbed an ankle, while Sheriff Stone grabbed the other. They yanked the bat off the top rail and flung the creature across the washroom, smashing it into the large mirror over the sinks.

The sheriff shot the thing in the chest, the boom deafening in the restroom. The bat flailed its wings in a death throe then rolled off the counter and flopped on the wet floor.

Miguel knocked on the door. “You can come out now. It’s dead.”

The stall door flew open. Maria and Sophia rushed out to escape the overflowing toilet.

“Are you guys okay?” Miguel asked.

“Thank God, Miguel you got here in time.”

“What’re you two doing in here?” Miguel looked down at a brown clump floating by his foot. “Sophia, did you do that?”

“It was an accident.”

“Where’re Betsy and Tess?” Miguel asked Maria.

“Last I saw, they were in the theater.”

“I need you and Sophia to get out of here as fast as you can,” Miguel told Maria.

While Maria and Sophia raced for the front entrance, Miguel and the sheriff bolted into the auditorium.

The projection lamp was no longer illuminating the white screen. The only source of lighting was the red exit sign over the door up front by the stage and a sliver shining out through the projection booth porthole.

Sheriff Stone hollered up, “Bron, you all right up there?”

Bron put his face up to the small opening. “Yeah, I’m okay. There was one up here but it got away. Killed Ernie Whitehead.”

Miguel gazed around the dark theater. He could hear hushed voices and children whimpering.

“It’s okay,” the sheriff called out to everyone. “We’re going to get you all out of here. Just sit tight.”

“Ahools have keen eyesight unlike smaller bats,” Miguel said. “Shine a light directly in their faces, it will temporarily blind them.”

“Like a deer in the headlights.”

“Exactly.”

Sheriff Stone handed Miguel his flashlight.

Rather than turn the flashlight on right away, Miguel strained to listen for the bats, which weren’t difficult to hear. Their wings rubbed continuously against their bodies sounding like autumn leaves rustling in a tree and they kept making a chattering noise like their teeth hurt.

Judging by the sounds, a creature was down the aisle by the stage and another one to Miguel’s right. He headed down the sloping aisle. As he drew closer, he could hear what sounded like laundry sloshing inside a washing machine. “Get ready,” he whispered to the sheriff.

Miguel switched on the flashlight.

A giant bat stood on a dead person lying on the floor. Its snout was buried inside the stomach cavity, gobbling up ropey intestines. The bright light shined in its face.

“Take the shot,” Miguel hollered.

Sheriff Stone fired twice. The first bullet struck the creature in the chest, the second slug in the head. The ahool slumped on the ravaged corpse.

Miguel panned the light to his right. A megabat was perched on the seatback gazing down at two figures huddled on the floor. They turned to the light.

It was Betsy and Tess.

“Careful, sheriff...” the flashlight flickered and went dead.

The megabat screeched.

A small light appeared.

Miguel saw Betsy’s upraised arm. She held her cell phone so the illuminated screen shined up at the creature for Sheriff Stone to take the shot.

Two shots rang out in the auditorium. The megabat slammed against the wall, its giant wings spread open and tumbled over the seats.

Betsy coaxed Tess to go ahead of her on their hands and knees. They crawled out from under the dead bat sprawled across the seats.

The overhead lights in the theater came on.

A dozen more people appeared from hiding places, some giving the sheriff sheepish smiles and waves of gratitude as they scurried from the auditorium.

Bron bolted through the doorway. He ran up to Betsy and Tess and hugged them. “Thank God, you’re okay.” He turned to Miguel and Sheriff Stone. “Sorry I took so long to turn on the lights. I couldn’t find the panel.”

The sheriff stepped over to the dead woman slumped in a seat. He checked her pulse and found none. He walked up to the base of the stage. He gazed down at the brutalized body.

Betsy looked over at the sheriff. “They’re the Bickersons...”

Sheriff Stone shook his head. “No, it’s Ronald Keener. That’s his wife, Beatrice.”

“Sorry, sheriff, that must have sounded...” Betsy apologized.

“It’s okay.” He looked at Miguel. “Counting Ernie Whitehead, and Tina Harvey and Louie Fisher out in the lobby, we have five dead.”

“Six,” Bron said.

The sheriff turned.

“I found Denny Jameson upstairs. What’s left of him.”

“Damn and these things were supposed to be only a Level-2 threat. Guess that will have to change.”

Ever since the cryptids escaped from the zoo, a threat index had been established nationwide, similar to a hurricane warning system. Whenever a sighting was made or an attack was reported, an alert—the Cryptid Warning System, commonly called the CWS—was broadcasted warning people in the nearby region of the impending danger. A Level-1 being less of a threat ranging up to a Level-5 for the extremely dangerous creatures determined by categorizing past events and the number of people the cryptids injured or killed.

“Be thankful this wasn’t a five,” Miguel said. “Or there wouldn’t have been any survivors.”

14

PITSTOP

Since their narrow escape from the cabin, Jack and Nora had been on the road for close to ten hours, stopping only once to fill up the gas tank. Though tired and in much need of rest, Jack insisted they keep going, worried Connors' men were still on their trail and not far behind.

For Lennie, being confined in the moving van was worse than being stuck in a cage. At least in a cage, he could peer out between the bars. His only view of the outside world was the dim opaque rooftop skylight and the narrow sliding window behind the cab's seats, which Nora was currently peering through.

Jack glanced over at Nora. "Please tell me he's sleeping."

"No, he's..."

"Oh, jeez. Is he doing it again?" Jack hit the button on the armrest to lower his window only to have the fast-moving air outside suck the rank odor of feces into the cab past Jack's face. Like it or not, he was going to have to pull over somewhere and shovel out the back of the moving van.

"He can't help it."

"Well, he could have at least given us a sign."

"What, you want him to scratch on the door?"

"No, I just didn't expect him to eat everything back there."

"Yerens have a robust metabolism."

"A polite way of saying he's a gluttonous pig."

A hard thump pounded on the cab wall behind Jack's head.

"I think you hurt his feelings."

"Yeah, right."

They were headed down a two-lane countryside highway of vast olive tree groves and apple orchards. Rest stops every twenty miles, small agricultural towns in between.

Jack spotted a dirt service road running back along an irrigation ditch and pulled off the highway. He drove among the trees until he thought they were far enough away from being spotted and stopped the van. He turned to Nora. "If I let him out, think you can coax him back in?"

"Does a yeren crap in the van?"

"You're so funny." Jack turned off the engine. He opened the driver's door and jumped down. Nora got out on her side. They walked around to the back. Jack lifted the rollup door. The smell nearly bowled him over.

Nora covered her nose and mouth. "Lennie, come out." She waved to him with her other hand.

Unable to stand all the way, Lennie scooted across the leaves and hay on the cargo hold floor. He extended his huge feet over the rear bumper onto the ground. He kept his head low and climbed out. The twelve-foot tall yeren stood straight, stretching his long arms over his head. He sniffed the air, eyeing a nearby row of apple trees and lumbered toward them.

Jack noticed the green fruit. Either they were Granny Smith apples or they weren't ripe. The last thing he wanted was cleaning up diarrhea. "See that he doesn't eat too many."

Nora walked over to supervise the big oaf.

Jack climbed up in the cargo hold. He pulled a handkerchief out of his back pocket and tied it over the lower part of his face.

He grabbed a snow shovel hanging on the wall. He watched where he stepped, scooping and chucking large clumps of feces out into the orchard.

A few minutes later, Lennie ambled back.

Nora was walking behind him, prodding him with a big stick. "I managed to stop him from eating too many but I know he's still hungry."

"Maybe we can try a drive-thru. Order him fifty Big Macs."

"I don't think so."

"What do you suggest?" Jack waited for Lennie to climb back inside the back of the moving truck.

"No junk food. He needs to eat healthy."

Jack lowered the rollup door. "So what, we walk him into a Whole Foods?"

"Not exactly but close. I have another idea. We'll stop at the next town."

* * *

"Don't you think we're in enough trouble?" Jack couldn't believe he'd actually let Nora talk him into becoming a common thief. But there they were, sitting in the grocery market parking lot, waiting for an unsuspecting victim.

It only took twenty minutes before Nora exclaimed, "There, follow that pickup."

Jack started the moving van. He kept a fair distance and followed the truck filled with crates of fresh vegetables along the front of the supermarket. When it turned down the side of the building, Jack made sure to keep his distance. He stopped where the service road behind the store sloped down a ramp.

He watched the truck pull around and back up to the loading dock.

"Wait until the driver goes inside," Nora instructed.

A short man with black hair and a bushy mustache got out of the truck. He carried a piece of paper in his hand. He went up the concrete steps. He walked past a closed rollup door and entered through a doorway into the receiving area.

"Now!" Nora shouted.

Jack raced down the ramp. He turned sharply and backed up next to the truck. Nora was out before he could come to a complete stop. He watched her through the passenger side mirror as she went to the back and disappeared from view. He could hear the rear van door opening.

He glanced at the driver's side mirror. He could see Nora grabbing wooden produce crates and throwing them inside the van. He started to open his door to go back and help but she shook her head, telling him to stay where he was in case they had to make a quick getaway.

Lennie appeared beside the truck.

Nora turned to coax him back inside the van.

The giant yeren ignored her, grabbing two crates from the truck bed then disappeared from Jack's view.

Nora lifted out another crate...

The exact moment the owner of the truck stepped out. The man saw Nora, raised his fist, and yelled at her.

Jack stuck his head out the window. "Nora, get in here."

The angry man raced down the cement steps.

Nora threw open the passenger door and jumped in, slamming it closed.

Jack gunned the vehicle and raced up the ramp.

15

FIRE IN THE HOLE

Laney struggled with the long garden hose. It kept kinking and getting tangled, causing her to stop watering and hunt down the problem. She was hosing the azaleas when she heard a rumbling engine entering the parking lot. She turned off the nozzle and walked over to see who it was.

An old model car with wide chrome-rimmed tires and sporting a lime-green paintjob pulled up to the entrance. The driver revved the beastly engine and turned it off.

Toby Mack climbed out, a man in his seventies with a salt and pepper beard and one of her frequent customers. He stood by the open door, drumming his hands on the car's roof. "Well, what do you think?"

"Pretty fancy."

"Picked her up yesterday. Ain't she a beaut? You're looking at a 1970 V-8 hemi Plymouth Barracuda 440 with a Hurst linkage. She can do zero to sixty in 6 seconds flat. I know; I did it on the way over."

"Wow. Pretty impressive."

"I'll say."

"Given Alice a ride yet?"

"No, she doesn't...hey, how'd you know we'd hooked up?"

"She told me."

"Well, not like it's a secret. I mean the cat's out of the bag at the senior center."

"I see your hands are looking better."

Toby showed off his youthful-looking hands. "Hard to believe. Two months ago they were gnarly as crab legs."

"So I gather no more rheumatoid arthritis?"

"Gone, kaput. Elvis is no longer in the house."

"No more cane?"

"Nope. Or wheelchair. I'm even back to my morning walks."

"That's wonderful."

"I wouldn't be standing here if it weren't for you and your husband."

"We're just glad we can help people like yourself."

"You should do one of those start-up companies. Think of all the lives you could change."

"You know we can't do that, Toby."

"Afraid some pharmaceutical company will come and steal it from you?"

"Something like that, yes."

"I get it." Toby shut the door. He came around the front of the car, patting the hood like it was a trusty steed, an athletic bounce to his step.

They walked back to Laney's office. She unlocked her desk and handed Toby a plastic baggy containing the ground-up cure-all plant.

"I sure wish you'd let me thank that husband of yours."

"Someday."

"Well, I better get going. Promised Alice I'd take her shopping."

Laney walked Toby out to his car. "Drive safe. Say hi to Alice for me," she said as Toby got behind the wheel.

"Will do." Toby started the muscle car, slipped it into gear, and peeled out of the parking lot leaving behind a short patch of burnt rubber on the asphalt. He sped down the dirt road, the big tires kicking up a trailing plume of dust.

Laney shook her head and was about to head back into the nursery when she spotted a black SUV parked beyond the trees. She wasn't positive but it looked like a Ford Expedition, maybe a Cadillac Escalade. The windows were tinted so she couldn't see who was inside.

She turned her attention to the dirt road; the dust dissipating and settling to the ground. The Barracuda was likely to the main road by now.

She glanced back at the trees.

The SUV was gone.

* * *

Laney was cleaning the kitchen counter when she heard a rattling noise. She dropped the dishrag on the table and stepped into the small living room.

The doorknob twisted. Someone was trying to jimmy the front door.

She went back into the kitchen. She looked out the window over the sink and saw only her reflection in the glass. She heard footsteps outside in the darkness.

Laney flicked the wall switch. The kitchen went pitch black. She edged over to the stovetop. She grabbed a long-handled skillet.

The front door burst open.

She peeked around the corner.

Two silhouettes stood in the doorway. They had helmets with night vision goggles and wore black military-style uniforms. The intruders entered, panning their compact assault rifles about the living room.

Laney edged along the wall. She hid behind the refrigerator. She reached up and took down a large LED flashlight. She held the torch by the handle, her thumb poised over the button.

She waited for them to enter the kitchen. She knew she would get only one chance. The first man crept in, followed by the second man.

Laney shone the super bright light into their faces. The men recoiled, turning their heads, temporarily blinded by the powerful beam. She swung the frying pan, striking a man in the chin, shattering his jaw.

She ducked when the second man fired off a quick burst from his machinegun even though he couldn't see. Bullets riddled the cabinets, shattering glassware and porcelain dishes.

Laney kneecapped him with the skillet with a bone-crushing wallop.

Both men fell to the floor, withering in pain.

Laney dropped the skillet and bolted from the kitchen. She threw open the back door. She raced out of the cottage. Even though she had the flashlight, she chose not to use it for fear they might see her.

She had to warn Allen.

She dashed down the trail, hoping not to stumble and fall, the greenhouse visible a short distance ahead.

Laney rushed to the entrance and stepped inside; the interior dimly lit by luminous lichen framing the glass panels. "Allen, where are you?" Laney called out, stepping through the entrance.

"I'm right here." Allen stood ten feet back between the raised garden beds. He appeared somewhat human in the gloom.

"They found us."

"I know. I heard the shots. Move away from the door."

Laney rushed in. She heard voices outside, heavy boots trampling toward the greenhouse.

"Thank God you're okay," Allen said. He motioned for her to duck down behind a table as three commandoes charged into the greenhouse.

They opened fire and sprayed the indoor nursery, cutting down plants and blowing out glass panes. A steady stream ripped through Allen.

"NOW!" Allen yelled.

The man-eating tree sentries bent down, grabbing two men in their savage mouths, chomping their heads off below the shoulders.

The man stopped firing to reload. He fumbled for a fresh magazine, unable to take his eyes off of Allen who still remained standing. The puncture holes in Allen's body immediately sealed over. "You're going to have to do better than that."

Six men dashed inside and fanned out.

A palmetto lashed out, cutting off a man's leg with a razor-sharp blade.

Creepers ripped around ankles, taking two men down. Strangler vines wrapped around their necks and choked them to death.

A commando screamed, kicking his feet as a man-eating tree swallowed him.

Laney turned. A man was sneaking up on her.

Allen lunged with lightning speed. Laney felt her husband press his back against her chest to shield her. His skin was rock solid. She heard machinegun fire. Allen's body recoiled with every hit, preventing the bullets from striking her, his ossified body impenetrable like petrified wood.

Allen ripped off the man's helmet. A toxic sap shot from Allen's fingertips, blinding the gunman; the adhesive goop sealing his nose and mouth.

"Everyone out!" an authoritative voice yelled.

Three men managed to escape out.

Allen turned to Laney. "You have to get out of here, now."

"I'm not leaving without you."

"Laney, this is no time to argue." Allen ushered her to a hidden panel that opened up. "Now, go. Don't worry, I'll find you." He shoved her outside.

Laney stayed low and crept toward the trees. She glanced over her shoulder.

A commando wearing twin tanks strapped to his back approached the greenhouse entrance. Liquid fire dripped from the nozzle of his gun.

Laney yelled, "Allen! They have a flamethrower!"

A twenty-foot long stream of fire belched into the greenhouse. The operator fanned the blaze from side to side. In seconds, the indoor nursery became an inferno, the burning plants shrieking, glass panes cracking and falling into the scorching crematorium.

Allen in the middle of it all engulfed in flames.

Laney screamed, dropping to her knees.

She wept as they bound her hands behind her back and pulled a hood down over her head.

16

SURPRISE GUEST

Nick wasn't nervous sitting in front of a live audience as much dreading what might come out of Marty Mayer's mouth. He knew the talk show host was notorious for putting his guests on the spot even if it was just for a laugh. Lucas Finder had been a classic example. Waiting behind the curtain to be announced was beginning to seem like an eternity...

"Ladies and gentlemen, please welcome my next guest, survivor and author of *Cryptid Hell*, Nick Wells."

A stagehand pulled back the curtain. Nick walked out to a round of applause.

Marty got up from his desk to shake Nick's hand. "Welcome and make yourself comfortable, Nick." He waved graciously to the chair next to his desk and sat down.

Nick occupied the hot seat. "Thank you so much for inviting me on your show."

Marty held up the paperback for the camera so the audience could get a close-up of the book cover on the big screen. "So, what is the book about?"

"Well, it capitulates my family's horrific weekend at the theme park."

"Cryptid Zoo."

"Yes."

"Go on."

"At first it seemed like it was going to be a dream vacation. We were to stay in a plush 5-star hotel with an Olympic-sized swimming pool; everything free, meals included, all courtesy of Wilde Enterprises."

"Of which you were an employee," Marty said, putting the book down and sitting forward with his elbows on the desktop.

"Yes. I worked in marketing. It was my job, along with some of my fellow employees, to critique the facility for a promotion add campaign. That meant reviewing the restaurant and hotel, looking for services in need of improvement."

"Did that include the attractions?"

"It did."

Marty gazed at the book on his desk and picked it up. "I have to say, the book is very graphic."

"I felt it was my responsibility to let the public know what really happened and the terror we experienced that weekend."

Marty opened the book, revealing Post-its marking certain pages. He thumbed to one of the markers. "This is wild-" Marty grinned up at the audience "-No pun intended," which got everyone laughing. "There was actually a Kraken in the swimming pool?"

"Yes, that's right."

"Why would they put a sea monster in the pool?"

"They didn't."

"Then, how did it get there?"

"Somehow it got out of the aquarium; The Tank."

Marty laughed. "And took a stroll over to the pool?"

Some of the audience shared in the humor.

"You have to remember, this creature can—"

"By your account, this sea monster killed a lot of people."

The studio became deathly quiet.

Marty turned to another page. "This section about the hotel lobby is especially disturbing. Bili apes tearing off guests' arms and legs?"

"They're extremely violent. Believe me, they did worse things as you probably know from reading my book."

"Well, I think if a big ape tore off my arms and legs that would just about do it for me," Marty said, facing the camera with a big grin. He glanced back at the book and rifled the pages to the next Post-it. "Let's talk about Gabe."

Here it comes, Nick cringed.

"How is he doing by the way? You say here your son suffered a mental breakdown."

"Yes. He was quite traumatized."

"And what do you think sent him over the edge?"

"We're not quite sure. I believe everything that was happening just got to be too much for him. You have to remember we were in constant fear for our lives."

"Isn't there a history of mental illness on your wife's side of the family?"

"What?" Nick couldn't believe Mayer was actually blaming Gabe's condition on Meg's mother, who suffered dementia and died only last year. And how did he even know, if his producers hadn't dug up some dirt just to boost the ratings? He wanted to grab the son of a bitch by the throat and rip out his voice box. "I'd rather not discuss my son at this time."

"Well, you know Nick, I do have a big surprise for you."

"Oh, yeah. And what is that?" Nick looked up at the audience. Several of the people in the first row were leaning back in their seats, frightened looks on their faces.

Nick heard a loud roar behind him. A giant white furry hand came down on his shoulder. Nick spun around in his seat.

An eight-foot tall yeti towered over him.

He didn't mean to but he screamed. He scooted out of his chair, falling backwards onto the floor.

The Nepal monster opened its huge mouth and roared again.

Expecting the yeti to pick up the chair and toss it, Nick did a comical crabwalk in front of Marty's desk, evoking raucous laughter from the audience.

Nick glanced up at Marty.

The talk show host was still in his chair. Marty looked at the abominable snowman and clapped his hands. "Unbelievable!"

A young man stepped out from behind the giant creature. He held a black box with a control pad. He threw a switch and the robot bellowed.

Marty stood up and gestured to the animatronics yeti. "You're all getting a sneak peek of the creature created by Burt Owen's Horror Workshop that will be featured in the new exciting monster movie coming out this summer: *Beast of the Himalayas*."

Nick got to his feet slowly, feeling the fool. Everyone seemed too awestruck with the monstrous yeti to pay him much mind. At least, that is what he hoped. He didn't know what was worse: becoming a laughingstock in front of everyone on nationwide television or being ripped limb from limb by a Siberian snow creature.

Either way, he wanted to bury his head in the sand.

17

SPINNING WHEEL

Milo Brown promised himself he would travel once he graduated from high school. Even though his parents were hoping he would further his education attending a reputable university, Milo knew he would never be happy sitting in classrooms when he could be out exploring the world. He thought it would be fun to fly to Europe and hitchhike everywhere. But when he tallied the cost of airfare, lodging, and other expenditures, he realized he didn't have enough money saved up from his summer jobs.

Despite his parents' objections, Milo decided to take a dry run and hitchhike the length of his home state. His mother had been especially concerned about his safety accepting rides from strangers that might be psychopaths and serial killers. Milo assured his mother he could take care of himself. He had a green belt in karate and worked out regularly with weights in his room. Plus, he had a canister of pepper spray and a Swiss army knife in his backpack. Just dare anyone to mess with him.

What he didn't realize was the amount of walking involved when hitchhiking. Not many people were willing to give a scruffy-looking teenager standing on the side of the road a lift. Especially out in the middle of nowhere. From where Milo stood, there wasn't a gas station or building in sight. Just open desert. Nothing but blue sky and a flat landscape of rough terrain and scattered sagebrush as far as the eye could see.

And a long stretch of two-lane highway that tapered off in the distance in each direction. It had been almost two hours since he had last seen a car or truck drive by.

He reached back and pulled the plastic water bottle from a pouch in his backpack.

Unscrewing the lid, he tipped the bottle back. A few drops dribbled into his mouth. He was completely out of water.

He gazed up at the sun, shielding his eyes. He wasn't certain of the exact temperature but it had to be in the three digits.

Maybe he should have listened to his parents. Sitting in an air-conditioned classroom didn't sound so bad right about now.

Milo had some snacks in his pack: a melted Hershey bar, some salted peanuts, a crushed bag of sea salt potato chips, and a half-eaten granola power bar. He could have had a backpack full of food but it wasn't going to do him a bit of good if he didn't have water.

Before starting his little adventure, Milo thought he should know a few basics about surviving the outdoors. Like how long a person could go without water? In normal conditions, he might stay alive for three to four days, but that was stretching it. In this heat and with no shade, he was lucky to make it two before he became completely dehydrated and his throat closed up.

He contemplated lying down in the middle of the road, pretending to have passed out the moment he heard a vehicle approaching. But when he placed his hand on the asphalt it was so hot it burned his palm. He blew on his skin to cool it off. It was probably just as well. It was doubtful a driver would even see him in the wavering haze and stop in time before running him over. The last thing he wanted was to become roadkill like the jackrabbit pancake he'd passed a couple of miles back.

Milo stared down the endless strip of shimmering asphalt. He could see something coming towards him down the middle of the road.

It wasn't a car or a truck.

He had to blink a couple of times. Surely it was a mirage. Since when does a tire roll down the road all by itself? But that's what it looked like; a spinning wheel out for a desert jaunt.

He didn't know what to make of it. He stepped over to the shoulder of the road so as not to be in its path and get run over, figuring it was going to keep on going.

It came to a rolling stop ten feet away from where Milo was standing.

"Holy shit!" Milo couldn't believe what he was seeing.

The fat snake released its thin tail from its mouth and stood up like a cobra. It was enormous and had to weigh a hundred pounds if not more and had a series of dark rings on its body.

The large head was slightly beveled, its black eyes fixed on Milo.

He took a step back and to the side. The ebony globes stayed on him like twin tracking beams. He knew if he tried to run, the serpent would be on him in a flash.

The strange-looking reptile opened its mouth, exposing four-inch long venomous fangs and let out a forceful hiss. Milo stared at the vicious teeth and his stomach dropped into a bottomless pit. His heart pounded in his chest like a bomb about to explode. The sweat streaming down his back was no longer from the heat but sheer panic, chilling his spine.

Why hadn't he listened to his parents?

He turned to run.

The giant snake lunged...

Milo heard a loud splat. He looked back and saw a white moving van come to a screeching halt. The passenger door flew open. A woman stepped out of the cab. She ran up to Milo. "Are you okay?"

"Yes, I think so."

A man came around the front of the vehicle. "Did he get bit?"

"It didn't bite you, did it?" the woman asked.

"No."

"Thank God. I'm Nora and that's Jack. What's your name?"

"Milo. What was that thing? Do you know?"

"That was a tzuchinoko. It's a Japanese cryptid. I'm guessing it escaped from the zoo."

Milo heard a pounding from inside the back of the moving van.

Nora turned to Jack. "It has to be sweltering back there."

Jack walked to the rear of the vehicle. He grabbed the bottom of the rollup door and shoved it up on the track.

Milo followed Nora to the back of the van. He took a look inside and yelled, "Oh my God. What is that?"

A giant ape-like creature with long orange hair was sitting in the cargo hold.

"Don't be afraid. Lennie won't hurt you."

"Is that an orangutan?"

"Lennie's a yeren. I take it you've never seen one before?" Nora asked.

"No."

Nora waved her hand, beckoning the large animal to come out of the van. Lennie scooted across the floor and climbed out.

Milo hadn't realized how huge the yeren was until he saw it standing. It had to be over twelve feet tall. The arms were longer than Milo's height. Lennie took a couple of steps on the hot asphalt but it didn't seem to bother him as he had thick, black padded soles on his feet.

Jack kept a vigilant watch for cars, looking one way then glancing down the opposite stretch of road. "We should get going. I don't like being out here in the open."

"Can I get a lift from you guys?" Milo asked.

Jack looked at him. "That might not be a good idea."

"Jack, we can't just leave him here."

"Nora. It's too dangerous."

Lennie stared at the back bumper and growled.

Milo squatted so he could see under the van. The huge snake was wrapped around the axle. “Guys. I think that snake is still alive. It’s moving.”

“Don’t anyone move.” Jack walked to the driver’s door and reached inside the cab. He came back carrying a large revolver. “Okay. You better stand behind me. Nora, get Lennie out of the way.”

Nora walked up to the big ape-man. She placed her hands on his belly and pushed, instructing him that she wanted him to move. He stepped back. He kept going until Nora had directed him onto the shoulder of the road.

Jack knelt and leaned down. He extended his arm, aiming the gun. Milo heard the hammer cock. The giant snake let out a menacing hiss.

The loud gunshot caused Milo to jump.

Lennie made a grumbling noise.

Jack tucked his gun inside his waistband. He went to the back of the van. He reached inside and took out the snow shovel. Using the scoop, Jack was able to unravel the dead snake from the axle.

Milo heard the thick body flop on the asphalt.

He watched Jack lay down the shovel and reach up into the wheel well.

“I don’t believe it. Damn!” He held up a black magnetized box the size of a pack of cigarettes for everyone to see.

“What’s that?” Milo asked.

“It’s a GPS car tracker.”

18

PICNIC CRASHERS

Abe unscrewed the dome light in his cruiser so he could leave the front doors open without draining the battery. He made sure the riot shotgun wasn't loaded and locked in its mount at the base of the front seat. A plastic overlay of the Rocklin Falls Sheriff Department screen saver was taped to the monitor on his computer screen.

He stepped out of his car and looked around at the other emergency vehicles on display for the picnic.

The town's fire department had brought out the red antique fire truck from storage and polished it up. It was nothing more than a long-bed pickup truck with ladders strapped along the fenders and fire axes hanging behind the cab doors.

A large truck from the Forest Service was parked by the edge of the tents with emergency supplies and tools laid out on tarps for exhibition. Bron Banner saw Abe gazing his way and gave the sheriff a wave.

"Looking good," Abe hollered.

A paramedic ambulance had its back doors open and was available for people to inspect. Two technicians were standing by to answer questions and respond to any medical emergency that might arise during the event.

Another added attraction was a search and rescue helicopter that could be easily modified to a medevac aircraft as the tail rotor was housed in a sound-reducing plastic shroud, lessening the noise so it could land at hospital heliports and not disturb patients or neighboring communities. The gray and red aircraft had three rotary blades, a glass-front nose, a sliding side door, and seating for five passengers. The pilot sat inside the cockpit with the door open, reading a paperback.

A Channel 8 News van was parked near the entrance. News of the ahool attack at the movie theater had spread fast, getting national attention. Abe spotted Jenny Lee standing with her news crew ready to interview people as they came from the parking lot and passed through the gate into the picnic area.

Abe walked out into the clearing. He waved to Charlie Dexter aloft in a cherry picker. Charlie had a hunting rifle cradled over the crook of his arm. He waved back. Abe glanced around and saw the other three lookouts at their posts.

He could hear the locals' friendly voices and laughter as they gathered under the tents and the corrugated roof over the dining area. The permeating aroma of meat cooking on the grills made his mouth water.

It was good to see the community getting together. He hoped there was a big turnout. Abe and those helping with the event had taken extra precautions to ensure everyone remained safe and had a good time.

He went over to the tables lined up under a tented canopy.

Clare was standing behind a table. She had pamphlets laid out with literature about her business. Two of her goats were hitched to the table leg.

"Better watch they don't stampede and run off with your table."

Clare reached inside a feedbag. She threw some pellets on the ground. The goats dipped their heads and scooped up the dry food with their lips. "I think they like it here just fine."

"I thought you'd bring Rounder."

"He's home, minding the farm." Clare looked over at the woman seated next to her with an array of tubs and blocked cheeses arranged on the tabletop. "Myrtle and I were just talking. She thinks we should go into a joint venture." Myrtle was known for her delectable dairy cheeses and had won 1st place blue ribbons from just about every county fair in the state.

"Don't you think watching them eat...is a lot simpler than pulling a teat?"

Myrtle laughed. "Abe Stone, aren't you the laureate."

"Sorry, that sounded better in my head."

"Oh, there you are."

Abe turned and saw Miguel walking towards the table. "Hey, Miguel," Abe smiled. "Where's your family?"

"In line, getting their food."

Abe glanced out across the clearing.

No one was standing on the cherry picker platform.

"Where did Charlie go?" Abe stepped out from under the tent.

Miguel walked alongside. "That's strange. He wouldn't just leave his post without someone relieving him."

A dark shadow loomed over them.

Abe looked up and had to shield his eyes from the bright sun. Something was falling out of the sky right above their heads. "Look out," Abe shouted and pushed Miguel out of the way.

It sounded like a wet, gravelly sack of cement hitting the ground.

"Ah jeez." Abe stared at Charlie Dexter's ruined body splattered on the dirt.

A loud squawk sounded overhead.

Abe looked up again.

The thunderbird had to be a hundred feet in the air. Damn thing had snatched up poor Charlie and dropped him from that height, a trait thunderbirds used to kill their prey before coming down to feast on the mangled body.

The lookouts from the other cherry pickers spotted the massive bird circling the picnic grounds and were taking potshots at it.

The thunderbird swooped down.

Abe pointed to the tents. "Tell everyone to take cover."

Miguel began yelling for people to stay where they were but some of them sensed they were in danger and began to scramble away from the picnic tables.

Pulling out of its dive, the thunderbird clutched the top of a tent and pulled the canopy up with its sharp talons, yanking out the tent pegs and knocking over the supporting poles. The monstrous avian let loose of the cover and flew up.

Abe drew his handgun but knew the mammoth bird was too far away for an effective shot. Thunderbirds' overlaying feathers were so thick they were like impenetrable armored Kevlar vests. Which is why none of the lookouts posted on the cherry pickers could shoot the damn thing down.

The thunderbird circled the picnic grounds.

That's when Abe had an idea. He raced over to the helicopter. The pilot had been watching the bird circling overhead from the cockpit.

"I'll need you to start your engine," Abe told the pilot.

"Why? There's no way I'm flying after that thing."

"I don't want you to. Just do it when I tell you."

The pilot started throwing switches on a center panel between the two front seats.

Abe ran over to Miguel who was persuading people to stay put under the protection of the corrugated roof. "Miguel, help me with these sides of beef."

They each grabbed a large butchered rib shank from the table next to the grills.

"What are we doing with them?" Miguel asked.

"Follow me." Abe charged over to the helicopter. He contemplated stacking the meat on top of the rotor hub but decided against it figuring they would only fall off from the vibration once the blades began to spin. He decided to place his on the ground five feet away from the aircraft.

He motioned for Miguel to put his slab of meat on the other side of the cockpit.

"What now?" Miguel asked.

"Let's see if it takes the bait."

The thunderbird wheeled overhead. Its keen eyes must have spotted the offerings because it was banking in a downward spiral.

"Fire it up!" Abe yelled to the pilot.

The engine whined and the rotaries began to spin. The blades revolved, gaining momentum, spinning so fast they gave the illusion of being invisible. The hub enclosing the tail rotor diminished most of the noise.

Abe saw the thunderbird swoop down into a dive. He grabbed the pilot by the arm and yanked him out of the cockpit. "Run for cover!"

Once under the tent, Abe turned and saw the magnificent bird pull up and hover over the helicopter. It looked like a gargantuan peregrine hawk, twelve feet long from the tip of its beak to the end of its black-feathered tail with a twenty-foot wingspan.

The predatory bird went for the bait, lowering its talons to grab a slab of meat off the ground.

Its feet caught in the whirling blades causing the bird to twirl around like it was being pulled down into a whirlpool. A wing dipped into the twirling rotors, shredding the limb, feathers and bloody flesh flying everywhere as the shrieking bird was cut into pieces.

Encumbered by the decimated creature, the engine quit suddenly causing the aircraft to shudder and lift a foot off the ground. The bent rotaries came to an abrupt stop, one blade still embedded halfway through the thunderbird's carcass.

Bron and a paramedic ran out into the clearing towards Charlie's prone body while the other paramedic drove the ambulance over. Abe watched while they covered the corpse with a blanket.

The pilot stared at his gore-covered helicopter. "Nothing like an all-purpose slice-and-dicer."

"Sure made a mess of your chopper," Abe said.

"I can't believe you said that with a straight face."

The paramedics looked over at Abe. He signaled for them to load the body in the back of the ambulance. The last thing he wanted was the news crew rushing over to film.

But then he realized he was too late.

Jenny Lee and her cameraman were making a beeline toward the ambulance.

Bron saw the two coming and helped the paramedics with Charlie's body.

Abe was relieved to see the ambulance's rear doors closing just as the Channel 8 News team ran up.

Jenny Lee said something to Bron but was too far away for Abe to hear.

Bron shook his head.

She asked him another question.

This time Bron nodded and pointed in Abe's direction.

"Ah, crap." The reporter was running his way.

* * *

Miguel watched the ambulance leave the picnic grounds discreetly with no siren or flashing lights and drive out through the main gate.

A few of the event volunteers were going around, shoveling chunks of the thunderbird into pushcarts used for collecting trash bags. One of them even joked about throwing some pieces on the grill but it was a tasteless joke at best and no one laughed.

He doubted if anyone would have enjoyed the meal knowing they were eating something that had killed someone from their community.

As not many people had witnessed Charlie's actual death—and thankfully his body had been removed—no one saw any harm in continuing with the picnic festivities.

Soon everyone was back at their tables, eating their food and enjoying the get-together.

Miguel didn't think ill of his neighbors. Even though a cryptid attack was always imminent and a constant threat, people still needed to be entitled to live their lives.

He walked over to check on Maria and Sophia. They were sharing a table with Betsy and Tess. "How are you guys doing?"

Maria gave her best smile despite what had just happened. "The girls were facing the other way," she said, letting him know they were spared seeing Charlie fall to his death. Miguel turned just the same and looked in the direction of the clearing, and the helicopter, which was hidden behind the backdrop of one of the tents. He could see dark splotches on the other side of the thin canvas. Blood splatter from the thunderbird.

"Save me a burger."

"Where are you going?" Maria asked.

"Check with the sheriff. I'll be right back." Miguel weaved through the picnic tables and went out behind the tents.

Jenny Lee was holding a microphone up to the sheriff's face. A burly cameraman was recording the interview. As soon as the reporter saw Miguel approaching, she turned her attention to him. “Excuse me but aren’t you Miguel Walla?”

“That’s right.”

“You’re the cryptid hunter. The one that caught those animals for the zoo.”

“Well, we didn’t actually catch them. Most of them were created in a laboratory. We just supplied samples.”

“Didn’t you have a partner? Jack Tremens?”

“Yes.”

“And where is he now?”

“I couldn’t say.”

“Couldn’t or wouldn’t?”

Sheriff Stone cleared his throat. “If you don’t mind, I would like to see how my wife is doing.” He walked off and headed for the tents.

Jenny Lee watched him leave then turned to Miguel.

“If it’s okay with you, I’d like to get back to my family.” Miguel was about to turn when he heard a woman scream. He gazed over at the parked cars.

A woman was running toward the main gate.

An enormous creature was right on her heels. It had short, tan hair with a thick, brown mane running down its spine. The broad shoulders were muscular like a bull as it ran on all fours. The thing had to weigh over three hundred pounds. It was like watching a lion chasing down an antelope, only in this case, it was a frightened woman fleeing for her life.

Even though Miguel had never come in contact with such a creature, he knew what it was having seen a picture on a cryptozoological chart.

The bear-dog caught up with the woman and leapt on her back, shoving her face down in the dirt. It held her down with its massive paws. Lowering its black-faced snout, it bit down, ripping a bloody chunk out of the woman’s back. It tilted back its head revealing vicious teeth as it swallowed the raw meat.

A man ran over carrying a rifle. He stopped to take aim at the creature.

Another bear-dog jumped out from behind a car. It landed on the hood, and with one powerful swipe of its paw, sliced the man’s face with its razor-sharp talons. Blood splashed onto the dirt as the man fell to the ground.

Miguel heard the chain-link fence rattle.

A bear-dog was actually scaling the fence with its hooked claws. For being such a big animal, it had the agility of a feral cat climbing a tree.

Sheriff Stone had retrieved his shotgun from the police cruiser. He ran toward the intruder climbing the fence. He fired but most of the pellets either passed through the open mesh or pinged off the metal fence. Before he could pump another cartridge into his weapon, the bear-dog was up and over the barrier. It bolted for the picnic tables.

Miguel saw the other two bear-dogs heading for the main group of people.

God, it was going to be a slaughter.

He watched in horror as a bear-dog charged a group sitting at a table. Before anyone could swing their legs off the bench, the savage animal was lashing out, inflicting horrendous wounds upon the picnickers. A man went backwards on the cement, his hands clutching his rendered stomach as his guts spilled out. Two people tried to flee. They were brought down by the vicious creature and ripped apart.

This thing wasn't killing for food, Miguel thought. It was killing because it enjoyed it. Like it was programmed to cause as much bodily harm to a human being as possible.

The other two bear-dogs ran into the crowd desperately trying to escape the savagery. The creatures chased down their prey like killing machines, brutally ending one life only to chase after another person.

Miguel saw Maria and Sophia huddling behind a table with Betsy and Tess. They were trapped with nowhere to go, surrounded by the carnage and forced to listen to the high-pitched screams. He was relieved to see some of the men had run out to their trucks and were returning with guns.

A bear-dog spotted Maria's group and jumped across the tables.

Miguel knew they didn't stand a chance. He looked over at the barbecue grills. He spotted a long two-prong fork next to a meat cleaver. He grabbed both utensils.

Hoping to surprise the bear-dog, Miguel stayed low and crept over, never once taking his eyes off the creature stalking his family. It was atop the table, staring down at the women and girls, ready to pounce. As there was so much noise and confusion, he was able to sneak up on the beast.

He could see Sophia and Maria's frightened faces between the bottom of the tabletop and the bench.

With an upward thrust, Miguel drove the barbeque fork into the bear-dog's ribs.

It howled and spun around.

Miguel swung the meat cleaver, severing the creature's left ear and slicing a long sliver off its face. It shook its head, tossing blood onto Miguel.

Recoiling with pain, the creature leaped off the table.

Miguel heard the welcoming sound of sporadic gunfire.

The screaming had died down. Miguel gazed around. He couldn't believe the butchery. There had to be thirty people lying on the ground. The blood-soaked concrete looked like a collecting drain from a slaughterhouse.

He looked beyond the clearing and saw the bear-dogs retreating through the main gate. Another creature was waiting by the cars. He watched the four bolt into the nearby woods followed by men running after them with guns, firing haphazardly to scare them away.

Miguel cringed when Jenny Lee approached, followed by her cameraman.

She took a moment to assess the bodies like a war correspondent and showed little emotion like she saw this kind of thing everyday. "You are getting this, right?" she said to the cameraman.

"Come on, have a little decency," Miguel said, shoving the camera out of the way.

The hard-nosed reporter didn't flinch. "Mr. Walla. Tell us, what do you know about these creatures and how long has it been since they escaped from the zoo?"

"They didn't."

"What?"

"There were no bear-dogs in Cryptid Zoo."

"So where in the world did these creatures come from?"

Miguel shook his head. "I have no idea."

19

DETOUR

Jack pulled up to the curb in front of the Greyhound bus depot. He put the gearshift lever on the steering column in park but left the engine idling. “Well, Milo, this is as far as we can take you.”

Milo reached for the handle on the passenger door then looked over at Nora sitting beside him. “I really want to thank you guys.”

“You’re welcome,” Nora said. “Here, take this for bus fare.” She handed Milo some money.

“I can’t take—”

“Don’t worry about it,” Jack said. “We always keep a little extra cash on hand for special emergencies or when we can help someone out.”

“Thanks.”

Milo began to open the door then paused. He turned to Nora. “Lennie doesn’t belong to you, does he?”

“Maybe not legally but I did raise him.”

Jack leaned forward on the steering wheel so he could see Milo. “There are some very unsavory people that want to get their hands on Lennie and put him on display.”

“What, stick him in a cage?”

“I’m afraid so. Do us a favor and don’t speak to anyone about this.”

“I won’t. I promise, Jack.”

“Good. You better get going.”

“Your parents are probably worried sick about you.” Nora gave Milo a friendly pat on the arm. “You take care.”

“I will.” Milo swung the door open. He jumped down to the sidewalk and closed the door. He gave Jack and Nora a wave, turned, and headed for the main entrance of the bus depot.

Jack threw the van into gear and pulled away from the curb. He glanced at the instrument panel. “We’re getting low on gas.”

“There’s a station up ahead.” Nora pointed to a convenience store with gasoline pumps on two islands in front.

Jack pulled in and parked at the pumps closest to the road. "Make sure Lennie stays quiet as a mouse."

Nora opened the sliding window behind the seat and peeked in the cargo hold.

Lennie shifted his weight in the back causing the van to rock from side to side. Once the vehicle stopped moving, he pressed his face into the opening. He opened his mouth and breathed out.

Jack turned away, covering his nose. "Get that boy some Listerine."

"Maybe when you're inside, you might pick him up a toothbrush."

"Yeah, right." Jack got out the driver's side. He walked around the front of the van and went inside the store.

A young woman in her early twenties was standing by the register, watching a small television on the counter.

Jack pulled down the bill on his ball cap to conceal his face from the surveillance cameras mounted on the ceiling. He handed the clerk four twenty-dollar bills. "Can I get eighty on pump number two?"

Instead of taking the money, the woman said, "Have you been watching this?"

Jack gazed at the small screen. The camera was panning on what looked like a picnic area with bodies everywhere. He couldn't believe they were showing so much bloodshed on a daytime broadcast. He would have thought the producers would have at least edited out the repulsive graphic scenes of violence. "Where did this happen?"

"I'm not sure. This just came on."

"Have they said what attacked those people?"

"The reporter said something about bear-dogs."

"Bear-dogs?" Jack knew what they were but had no idea where the creatures might have originated from.

"Here she is now," the clerk said, pointing to the woman appearing on the screen.

"So far we have seventeen people confirmed dead and twenty-two taken to the hospital, thirteen critical with life-threatening wounds. This is now officially the second worse attack after the Cryptid Zoo tragedy. Hunting parties are being formed as I speak to track down these vicious creatures that claimed so many lives today. A terrible end to what was supposed to be a joyous gathering of friends and neighbors. This is Jenny Lee, reporting from Rocklin Falls, California."

"Jesus," Jack blurted. That was Miguel's hometown. "Here, eighty on two." Jack shoved the money at the clerk and rushed out.

By the time he reached the pump, the numbers on the dial were clearing to zeros as he removed the handle. He twisted off the gas cap and inserted the nozzle. He went over and opened the driver's door.

Nora looked down at him. He could tell she knew something was up by the look on her face. “There’s been a change in plans,” he told her.

“I didn’t know we had a plan.”

“Something terrible has happened where Miguel and his family live. There’s been an attack. It was on the news.”

“Are they all right?”

“I don’t know. We need to go there.”

“But what about Connors? Surely that’s the first place he’d expect us to go.”

“Screw Connors. I need to make sure my friends are okay.”

“That’s about a six-hour drive.”

“Not the way I drive.”

* * *

“Damn, I don’t believe it.” Jack slapped the top of the steering wheel.

“Relax, Jack. It’s only a detour.”

They’d been making good time and had almost covered half the distance to Rocklin Falls when they got stuck behind a long line of stalled traffic in a road construction zone.

“What’s the hold up?” Jack rolled down his window. He stuck his head out and saw a flagman holding a sign, standing on the side of the road a couple of car lengths away. The sedan in front of them edged up as the vehicle in front of it moved forward ten feet then stopped abruptly.

Nora scooted next to Jack and called out through the open window to get the flagman’s attention. “Excuse me.”

“Yeah?”

“Is there an accident up ahead?”

“We have a crew repairing the road. We’re only able to let one car through at a time on the shoulder.”

“So what’s taking so long?” Jack asked.

“It’s been a losing battle. Every time we fill where the road collapsed, another part caves in.”

“Is it a sinkhole?”

“No. My boss thinks we’re on top of a fault line. Stupid surveyors.”

Jack noticed the driver in the car ahead of them, opening his door. He got out of the sedan and stepped away from his car, gazing down the long line of vehicles.

The flagman turned to the looky-loo. “Sir, I’ll have to ask you to get back in your car. You’ll be moving shortly.”

“What’s the damn holdup?”

"Sir, for your own safety. Please get back in your car."

Jack felt the van shake. He turned to Nora. "Make him stop."

Nora turned and slid open the window behind the seats. She peered inside the cargo hold. "Jack, it wasn't Lennie. He's fast asleep."

"Was that an earthquake?"

Dirt and rock exploded out of the ground in a large plume of dust, creating a massive crater under the two cars in front of them. The vehicles slipped into the deep pit.

The impatient driver lost his footing and fell into the abyss, screaming.

The flagman knew better than to get too close and backed away. He looked at Jack and yelled, "Get back or you're next."

Jack glanced in his side mirror. He saw a long line of cars behind them. They were boxed in.

Something tubular and long rose out of the crater. Its body was as big around as a ten-foot diameter pipe. The man that had fallen into the hole was hanging out of the creature's mouth, which was a circular pattern of spiked teeth. It shut its maw, the upper half of the man falling out of its mouth while the lower half slipped down its gullet.

"Oh my God, Jack."

"How did it get so big? I mean, the ones that escaped the zoo were only twenty feet long. This has got to be three times that."

"That's the problem with Mongolian death worms. They just keep growing and growing. The more they eat, the bigger they get."

"We have to warn these people."

"How?"

"Tell them to shut off their cars. If there are more, they're going to be drawn to the surface by the sound of the engines."

Another mammoth death worm burst out of the ground, flipping over a car.

"We can't stay here. Hold on." Jack cranked the wheel and drove the van off the pavement onto the nearby field. He gunned the engine, staying parallel with the main road. The van bounced over the rough terrain, tossing Jack and Nora around in the cab.

Lennie pounded on the wall behind the seats.

A few people thought their chances would be better if they fled their cars, which proved to be unwise as two more giant worms popped out of the dirt. The sightless creatures detected the vibration of running feet and were able to surface and intercept those trying to get away.

Jack didn't know how long they could keep driving through the field. Each time they hit a dip he expected the front end to crash into a ditch or the van to go flying in the air and flip over whenever they went over a bump. He could hear Lennie yowling in the back getting tossed about the cargo hold. Any second they'd for sure blow a tire.

He glanced over at the roadside construction and saw the Mongolian death worms crushing people with their massive bodies. Cars slamming into one another trying to squeeze out of the line as the asphalt crumbled, leaving a massive gaping hole preventing the remaining vehicles from crossing.

"There's a way up." Nora pointed to a dirt farm road leading up to the main road.

Jack was slowing down to make the turn when a black helicopter swooped down right in front of them, narrowly missing the van.

Nora stared out the windshield at the aircraft. "Oh my God, Jack. It's them."

Glancing up, Jack caught a glimpse of *Wilde Enterprises* on the rear fuselage. He cranked the steering wheel and stomped on the accelerator. The van raced up the embankment back onto the tarmac.

He saw a junction up ahead.

Two black SUV's barreled down the side road toward the intersection.

Another similar vehicle partially blocked the road. Five military-types in black combat gear stood ready with automatic carbines. The point man fired off a short burst.

"Get down," Jack yelled, ducking onto the seat, expecting the barrage to strike the windshield. Instead, the bullets riddled the front grill, punching through the radiator and ricocheting off the engine block.

He looked up and saw the van drifting off the road. He tried to straighten the vehicle but the tires were already spinning out on the loose gravel.

The van went airborne, crashing into an irrigation ditch. The airbag in the steering wheel burst into his face, snapping his head back against the headrest. He opened his eyes and saw the white bag slowly deflate. His nose and cheekbones felt like he had been punched by a heavyweight prizefighter.

He looked over at Nora.

She was unconscious. She had a nasty cut on her forehead from hitting the passenger side window. Her airbag hadn't deployed but her harness seatbelt had prevented her from being propelled through the windshield.

Lennie roared from the back of the van.

Jack's head lulled against the headrest. He glanced out at the side mirror.

Two men were standing by with rifles.

Jack heard the rollup door open.

He saw a man fly out from behind the van and land on the other side of the road.

Lennie appeared in the mirror.

The angry yeren grabbed a man by the arm and slammed him up against the side of the van.

Two men with rifles advanced. They fired their weapons simultaneously.

Lennie stumbled back and fell to the ground.

Jack's head swooned. He yelled "No!" and passed out.

20

GRASSLAND

Abe knew he was wasting his time trying to talk her out of it. "I still don't think it's safe out there. Give it a few days until we catch these things."

"Always the worrywart. I'll be fine." Clare opened the gun cabinet. She took out her Steyr SSG Marksman. She made sure the caps were covering the lens of the high-power scope. She slipped the competition rifle inside a soft case along with a box of .308 Winchester cartridges and two detachable 5-shot rotary magazines.

Clare's father had been a state champion sharpshooter and taught her from an early age. Even though Clare never cared for hunting, it didn't stop her from killing a predator threatening her animals. She was a phenomenal shot. Abe watched her behind the barn one day; plug a penny dead center from 100 yards.

"I'd feel better if you wore your dad's Ruger."

"If you insist." She opened a drawer at the base of the gun cabinet. She took out a coiled belt with a holstered revolver and a box of .38 specials. She put the gun and the bullets inside a small travel bag.

"Sure you don't want me to check on you?"

"Abe, you have a town to watch after. Stop your worrying."

Rounder bounded into the room. He looked up at Clare pensively as if to ask what was keeping her so long. She got the message.

"All right. I'm coming." Clare smiled at Abe.

"How long will you be gone?"

"Well, figuring eighty goats and they want me to clear off two acres of bramble, I'd say five days."

"There's no talking you out of going?"

"Abe, I have a business to run. The sooner I get these munchers on the job, the sooner I'll be back cooking your supper. Until then, there's some fried chicken and a couple of steaks in the fridge. I think you can manage."

"Just be careful." Abe put his hand up to Clare's cheek and kissed her.

"Don't miss me too much."

Abe followed Clare out. He watched his wife open the door so Rounder could jump up in the camper truck's cab. She started the engine and gave him a wave. He could hear the goats blatting inside the twenty-four-foot long livestock trailer as she drove away down the drive.

He hated to think of her out there alone.

Sure she had Rounder but he wouldn't be a match against that pack of bear-dogs.

The last person to see the savage beasts in the woods had been Ronnie Blight and he swore he saw them hightailing it up the mountain. Abe hoped it was true because they would soon be out of the county and become some other sheriff's problem, and he could stop fretting about Clare.

But then again Ronnie had claimed seeing UFOs landing on his cabin and little green men dancing on his roof.

Abe was feeling a little hungry having not eaten breakfast.

Clare's cold fried chicken sounded pretty good right about now.

He headed back to the house.

* * *

Clare was thankful the property owner had gone to the trouble of running irrigation piping to staged water troughs and set up temporary fencing around the small parcel of land that needed clearing.

She swung the trailer around and backed it up to the gate. She got down from the truck. Rounder jumped out and ran alongside the trailer to begin working.

Clare gave Rounder the command to sit while she unhooked the rope strap holding the makeshift wire gate to the post. She walked it back into the corralled area and leaned it against the perimeter fencing.

She went to the back of the trailer and pulled out the metal ramp, dropping it on the ground. Next, she unlatched the left rear door and swung it out. She opened the right rear door and left it also extended as a deterrent.

Two thin metal waist-high barriers blocked the sub divided trailer, preventing the goats from rushing out. As soon as the goats felt the warm sun on their bodies they reacted, sounding like bawling toddlers wanting to be taken out of their playpen. Clare opened the left side first to release half of the goats. It took the teamwork between her and Rounder to make sure the animals didn't slip out around the back of the trailer and run off even though it generally wasn't a problem as goats felt more protected in a large group.

Clare waved her arms to direct the goats while Rounder moved from side to side to make sure none of them got past him. Once one side of the trailer was empty, she opened the other side to release the rest of the goats. The second bunch paraded out to join the herd.

"Come bye," Clare called to Rounder.

The large dog raced toward the flock, herding them in a clockwise direction so Clare could go over and pull back the gate. She stood on the field side and secured the wire gate to the post.

Walking out amongst the goats, Clare surveyed the acreage that needed to be manicured. The landscape was fairly flat, making it easier for Rounder whenever he had to move the herd along to graze a new patch of land. Clare dreaded working her goats on steep hillsides, as it was extra work for Rounder running up and down chasing after strays.

The property owner had plans to open up his land to a local rancher for cattle grazing so resorting to pesticides to remove the noxious weeds and bushes was out of the question. Using a tractor or backhoe would have only resulted in damaging what good grassland there was. Hiring goats that ate for work was the answer.

Clare assessed the surrounding foliage. She saw patches of poison oak, which would be harmful for cattle but wouldn't have any ill effects on her goats; thorny blackberry bushes with ripe fruit, musk thistles, and white flowered hawthorn shrubs, just the right height for her little grazers. The ground was smattered with yellow dandelions, green downy brome, and purple knapweed: not much of a meal for cattle or sheep but a smorgasbord for goats.

The most important benefits of her goats was that they did not like to eat grass and the weed eaters made excellent fertilizer, pooping everywhere, and aerating the soil with their tiny hooves.

Satisfied that she had estimated the five-day job correctly, Clare walked back to the gate and let herself out, leaving Rounder to mind the herd. She left the trailer where it was, leaving the ramp down but closing the twin doors.

After she unhooked the trailer, she drove to a spot she had already picked out that was slightly elevated and parked so she could keep an eye on the herd, especially at night.

She stepped up into the back of her camper, which had everything she needed: propane stovetop, a full mini cooler, pull down table and bench seat, a sound mattress, canned goods, and a cramped toilet stall with a shower.

All the comforts of home though she would miss the companionship of Abe.

It would only be for five days. Maybe he would swing by and pay her a surprise visit. Though she didn't see the need, she thought it best not to disappoint her husband if he should happen by. She reached into the travel bag and took out her father's gun. She strapped on the holster. Clare unzipped the gun case, took out the Steyr Marksman, and slapped in a magazine.

Five minutes later after boiling herself a hot cup of instant coffee, she was sitting outside on a lawn chair next to the truck, surveying the land, with an extremely accurate sportsman rifle resting across her lap.

21

BOOKSIGNING

Ben Larson was counting the days when his training was complete and he could be assigned his own delivery truck. He'd even considered quitting rather than ride with Dennis but he knew he would only be hurting himself. His trainer was pompous and a condescending bore. Not to mention lazy. Most times Dennis never moved his fat butt out of the driver's seat while Ben did the heavy lifting, unloading packages and boxes from the truck and getting signatures.

In Ben's eyes, Dennis was worthless deadweight and should have been laid off long ago, having no business training new employees.

Certainly upper management was aware. Wouldn't that be something after his probation was up, if they canned Dennis and handed Ben the keys.

Dennis cleared his throat and hawked a loogie out the opening as the driver's door was slid back. "This is our last delivery. Shake a leg trainee and we can knock off early."

He sped through the large shopping mall parking lot, turned down a ramp, and stopped at the twenty-foot tall rollup door.

Ben jumped out of the truck. He went over to a touch pad and punched in the security code as he was bonded with the shopping mall security. He watched the electric door rise slowly all the way up.

He stepped into the underground tunnel and stood by the touch pad on the other side of the door. He waited for Dennis to drive in but the man just sat there. "What's the deal?"

"Get in."

"I'm supposed to close the door once we're inside."

"Screw that. Takes too long. We'll be right back out. Lickety split."

"That's not how we're supposed to do it. They want it secured at all times."

"Quit arguing. Don't forget who's doing your evaluation."

"Fine." Ben waited for Dennis to pull up. He grabbed the handle so he could boost himself onto the step and into the passenger seat.

Dennis stepped on the gas, ignoring the 5-mile per hour posted speed limit.

They followed the service tunnel until they came to the appropriate loading dock.

Dennis backed the truck up to the receiving area.

When Ben got out, he didn't see any employees anywhere. It was kind of creepy being underground with no one around. He walked to the back of the truck and threw up the sliding door. He stepped into the cargo area. As it was the last delivery there were only four boxes left on the shelves.

He was in the process of using his barcode reader to scan the first box when he heard a loud thump and Dennis screamed from the other side of the closed door sealing off the cab. The 10,000-pound truck rocked like a moored boat in rough waters to the sound of heavy thrashing while a wild animal vocalized *pant-hoots* and Dennis screamed like a woman in excruciating labor giving birth to a bowling ball-sized baby.

Ben didn't know what to do. Should he go out there and help Dennis?

Hell no!

But then it was no longer an issue because Dennis stopped yelling.

Ben heard flesh being rendered from bone and wet slobbering. Something was eating Dennis with gusto, grunting after each bite.

Ben took a step back. The barcode reader hit the lip of a shelf and fell from his hand. The plastic device thudded to the floor.

Then came bone-chilling silence.

The truck swayed as the thing jumped out of the cab.

Ben turned. He reached for the strap to pull down the truck's back door.

A giant chimpanzee the size of a gorilla covered in Dennis's blood came loping out from around the side of the van. It had deep scars on its face and chest and was four hundred pounds of vicious, unrelenting terror.

The ferocious primate screeched when it saw Ben and leaped into the truck.

* * *

Nick thanked the bookstore manager for the complimentary cup of coffee from the snack bar as he finished preparing his table for the book signing.

He'd had an enlargement of the *Cryptid Hell* book cover made into a five-foot tall freestanding cardboard display at a Kinko's printing shop, which looked impressive next to the six-foot long table. The paperbacks were lined up in five rows, one copy slightly overlapping the one behind it. He had another full box of books under the table for restocking the table.

Free bookmarkers with the image of the book cover were on the table with his contact information in hopes of encouraging a fan base of followers wanting to know more about him and his book, along with Sharpie pens for autographs.

Two tins with wrapped cookies and sweets for anyone that wanted one.

Not wanting to come off too stiff and self-important, Nick chose to dress casual: red polo shirt, tan slacks, and a black pair of penny loafers. He wanted to appear approachable; a down-to-earth author that readers would feel comfortable to talk with.

He went around the table and sat in the folding chair provided. It was comfortable enough with a thin padded seat and back but he knew after sitting for the two-hour period he was being allotted, his back would ache and his butt would be numb.

He had a couple of minutes before the store was to open.

He watched shoppers through the front window, walking about the mall and browsing the window dressings. An expansive area was just outside the storefront with specialty kiosks—overly priced brand name cell phones mostly—and merchants with carts, selling cheap trinkets and novelty toys. Two escalators stretched up to the second level where a chest-high glass enclosed railing, meant to prevent children from falling to their deaths, curved along a walkway to a pedestrian footbridge arching to the second-floor stores on the opposite side of the mall.

A small group of people was waiting outside for the door to be unlocked. He hoped they were coming to buy his book.

Nick remembered when the leased space had been B. Dalton ages ago. The bookseller always had a section reserved strictly for horror books. He loved that he could find all his favorite horror writers in one spot. After they went out of business, the store became Waldenbooks for a brief time, then Borders, and later Barnes and Noble. Now the horror titles were obscure in the Fiction and Fantasy sections. He missed B. Dalton.

He took a sip of his coffee. He hoped he looked relaxed but couldn't help feeling a little nervous. He'd dropped Meg off at the Sears at the other end of the mall so she could do some shopping with plans to meet up for lunch at the Cheesecake Factory after he was done with the book signing. He was looking forward to a good steak and a couple of drinks.

The store manager was ready to let in the customers. He fumbled a moment with a set of keys then unlocked the entrance door. He smiled and held the door open for the patrons and greeted them as they filed into the store.

Nick watched the shoppers disperse in different directions.

A woman headed straight for the tables and chairs set up in front of the snack bar. The barista behind the counter smiled at the woman approaching.

Two teenage girls rushed toward the Young Adult section.

A fidgety man made a beeline for the restrooms.

Half a dozen people headed straight for Nick's table.

"Well, hello there. I'm Nick Wells. So nice of you—"

A shrill alarm echoed in the cavernous shopping mall.

Everyone turned to the sound.

"What's that, a fire alarm?" the woman ordering coffee asked, turning to the store manager a few feet away.

The store manager frowned. "It's the evacuation warning system."

"What?" Nick said with disbelief. "Don't tell me it's a drill?"

"If it is, we weren't made aware."

Outside, the ear-piecing noise continued.

The two teenage girls hurried over. "What do we do?"

"Head for the nearest exit," the store manager replied.

Nick's heart sunk as his perspective book buyers turned away from his table. He reached inside his shirt pocket and took out his cell phone. He'd have to tell Meg to meet him at the car. He punched in her speed dial number. She picked up on the second ring.

"Jesus, Nick what's going on?"

"Some kind of stupid evacuation. Of all the—"

"I heard a gunshot. My God, they're saying there's a shooter in the mall."

"Get out of there as fast as you can. Meet me in the parking lot." He jumped out of his chair, stuffing the phone in his shirt pocket. Everyone in the store was rushing toward the door leading out into the mall. An exit to the outside was three stores down.

Nick saw two mall security guards run by the kiosks and dash up the escalator, moving toward the second level floor.

He heard a muffled crack. Definitely gunfire.

The guards had their weapons drawn. A guard spoke into a radio receiver clipped to a lapel on his shoulder. He motioned to the other guard and they sprinted toward the pedestrian footbridge.

Nick stepped out from behind the table. The barista and two clerks were hustling toward the door. He looked out through the front glass.

A frantic group of terrified people stampeded across the footbridge from the other side, running toward the armed security guards.

A woman fell and a man stumbled over her, falling on top of her. No one bothered to stop and help. They kept running, stomping on the fallen pair. Frightened out of their minds.

And then Nick saw it. They had good cause to be scared; he'd be running for his life too, though it wasn't a mad gunman they were fleeing.

It was something much worse.

He knew, he'd seen what it could do at Cryptid Zoo. At least a man with a gun could be talked down. Not this. This was a creature not to be reasoned with. All it wanted was to maim and destroy with no remorse—a monstrous killing machine.

The Bili ape caught up to the last person in the group.

The man screamed.

The giant chimp flung him over the railing. Nick watched with horror as the man plummeted to his death, his head slamming onto the shiny polished floor and cracking open like a blood-filled gourd.

The primate picked up the woman lying on the bridge that had tripped and threw her over as well. She let out a short scream before her body smashed down on a merchant's cart.

The man that had stumbled over the woman made a feeble attempt to crawl away but the ape would have none of it. It swung the man headfirst into the glass railing. His skull cracked the glass, leaving a bloody smudge.

The guards couldn't get a shot with the people racing towards them. The primate used it to its advantage. It loped right behind the scampering crowd. Instead of taking down the nearest person, it charged a mall guard. Before he could shoot, the ape head-butted him in the face. Savage teeth ripped out a chunk of his throat. The guard crumbled to the floor.

The second guard fired twice. A bullet ricocheted off the handrail. The other struck the massive ape in the shoulder. It yowled but instead of running away, the amazingly strong creature ripped off the man's arm with the gun still in his hand and flung it.

Nick watched in astonishment as the severed appendage sailed across the mall like a Hail Mary pass, striking a large glass pane by the bookstore front entrance. The impact caused the contracted muscles in the fingers to release the gun as the arm flopped on the floor; the pistol spinning a few feet away.

That's when Nick realized the shrill alarm had stopped. He couldn't take his eyes off the gun. If he could slip out and retrieve the weapon, he might have a fighting chance of getting out alive.

He looked up.

Frightened people were scampering down the tiled stairwell between the up and down escalators. Tripping over one another, some tumbling down the moving metal steps of the escalator going down. Rather than remain trapped on the second level with the maniac beast, four people fled down the up escalator, doubling their steps.

The Bili ape charged down the stairwell on all fours, its massive arms thrusting brutish knuckles into the granite steps, totally fearless of self-injury, its only focus to kill everything in its path.

The store manager had been combing the store for customers and came rushing back to Nick's table. "Mr. Wells, why haven't you left?"

"Look for yourself." Nick nodded toward the window.

The Bili ape was on a rampage: smashing windows, upending merchants' carts, destroying anything that got in its way. It scattered a display of stuffed animals. Thinking they were alive, the primate took pleasure ripping each toy to shreds. It even put a stuffed lion's head in its mouth and bit it off. When it realized it was only fabric and stuffing, the ape spat it out in disgust.

Nick saw the store manager staring at the gun outside the glass entrance door. "If you're thinking of going out there, I'd reconsider."

The store manager looked at Nick. "Someone's got to stop that thing."

"You wouldn't get two feet."

"Hey, you're looking at a star athlete. I ran the 100 meters in college."

"You go out there, you'll wish you hadn't."

"I don't and more people are going to die."

"Don't be a hero."

The store manager ignored Nick and pushed the glass door ever so slowly, never taking his eyes off the monstrous chimp, which at the moment was smashing its fist through a plastic directory of the merchants' locations in the mall.

The man was on a fool's errand. Nick thought of pulling him back but that would have only drawn attention and alerted the ape. Better to watch and pray. Nick held his breath as the store manager opened the door wide enough to squeeze his body through...

"Hey! What was that alarm all about? And where is everyone?"

Nick turned.

It was the man that had come into the store and gone straight to the restrooms. He must have been in there taking a healthy crap.

"Keep your voice down."

"What?"

"Shut up, you loud-mouth!" Nick glanced back at the door. The store manager was already out scurrying for the gun. Nick found himself silently rooting him on like a fan in the bleachers at a track meet cheering for a runner. *Go, go, you're almost there.*

The store manager reached the gun and picked it up. He took a couple of seconds to familiarize himself with the weapon.

Two seconds that cost him his life.

Even Nick didn't see the Bili ape coming. The giant chimp tackled the store manager with such velocity they smashed through the plate glass window into the bookstore.

Nick immediately backed away and ran past some tables with the latest bestsellers. He ducked behind a tall bookcase. He leaned his head out. The store manager was dead on the floor, missing both his legs.

The ape was nowhere to be seen.

Then he heard, "Oh Jesus, oh Jesus..." It was the man running back to the restrooms. A door banged open followed by an echoing screech. Then there was another bang and the man let out an agonizing scream. Nick figured he must have tried hiding in one of the stalls and the ape busted down the door, cornering him over the toilet.

If Nick was going to get the hell out of the bookstore, this was the time.

But he had made the mistake of running almost to the back of the store. Now he had to cross the same ground as quietly as humanly possible. But what if he did make it to the door? There was a gaping hole in the storefront. What choice did he have?

He stepped out from behind the bookcase and had only gone ten feet when the knuckle-walker appeared, blocking his path. Shoulders bunched, brown marble eyes glaring at its next victim.

Nick didn't hesitate. He turned left and dashed down the aisle between the tall bookcases. He prayed the ape hadn't cut him off, waiting for him at the end of the aisle. Instead, Nick heard a crash as hundreds of books toppled to the floor, followed by another crash, and more cascading books. The super-strong ape was pushing over the bookcases into one another like knocking down a row of dominoes.

Nick ran down the gauntlet maze, dodging the careening bookcases.

Reaching the snack bar, Nick huddled behind the counter.

He could hear the big ape snorting, stomping about the store. It must have sniffed him out because it sounded like it was coming his way. Any second and the ape would be upon him. He gazed up at the barista station.

The massive ape stood on its hind legs to look over the counter.

Nick threw a full pot of scolding coffee into its face. The chimp reared back and howled, its black face bubbling blisters. It stormed off through the store.

Men were yelling outside. Nick heard the ape let out a loud whoop.

And then heavy machinegun fire lit up the store, bullets tearing through the place.

The barrage lasted for almost a minute then stopped.

All was quiet except for boots crunching glass.

"Is there anyone in here?" a voice called out.

"Here," Nick answered.

"You can come out. We killed it."

Nick got up. He walked through the debris to the front of the store.

Six SWAT officers with automatic carbines stood around the great ape. They must have shot it a thousand times.

"You hurt?" the lead officer asked.

"No. I need to make sure my wife is okay."

"Sure, pal. You better go around the other way. Less messy."

"Okay." Nick glanced over at his book-signing table. It was flat on the floor, his organized novels damaged and scattered. He could smell urine. The damn ape had pissed all over his books.

He turned right as the officer suggested avoiding having to see all the bodies. He hoped the Cheesecake Factory remained open. He could certainly use those drinks right about now.

22

BLUE RIDGE

Abe drove his cruiser up the narrow paved road through the dense forest of junipers and ponderosa pines. The smell of the crisp mountain air and pine needles wafted through his open window. It had been a while since he had visited the Blue Ridge campground. Last time Clare and he had been there they'd had a neighbor watch the goats so they could bring Rounder on the outing.

He fondly remembered camping under the stars with his wife, catching fat rainbow trout, and watching the big dog play in the stream. Best two days of his life.

He turned onto the service road leading to the Park Service check-in station. A sign was posted on the front of the small booth: SORRY, CAMPGROUNDS FULL. Abe drove into the campground. If he remembered correctly, there were close to fifty campsites.

He noticed canvas and nylon camping tents ranging from T-shaped 14-person cabin habitats to the family-size accommodating 8 people down to 2-person dome tents; the campground a collage of greens, blues, and tans. Each campsite had its own concrete picnic table, a fire pit, and a standup barbeque grill supported on a single metal pole.

Some visitors had brought travel trailers, fifth-wheels, pop up tent trailers, truck campers, as well as twenty-five-foot recreational vehicles that were parked in a specific area of the campground providing electrical hookups.

Everyone had different ideas of how to rough it in the great outdoors.

Abe gazed out his windshield and saw a teenage girl walking her golden retriever, someone hiking through the trees, three teenage boys tossing the Frisbee, families sitting around the picnic tables enjoying themselves.

Abe stopped his car. He glanced around looking for Bron Banner's utility truck.

He stared at a posted white sign with a red circle and a diagonal line with a bear's head in the center, its mouth wide open and a hand offering the animal food, warning folks: DO NOT FEED THE WILDLIFE.

He spotted Bron's truck next to the building that housed the restrooms and showers. The park ranger was tossing a bulging black trash bag into a dumpster.

Abe drove over and parked behind Bron's vehicle. He got out of the cruiser, taking a moment to twist side to side at the waist to get the kinks out of his back after sitting behind the wheel. He walked over to the dumpster.

"Morning, Bron."

The park ranger turned and smiled. "Hey there, Sheriff. What brings you out here?"

"I wanted to thank you for helping out at the picnic."

"Oh, you mean with Charlie Dexter."

"Yeah. Damn news reporters."

"Guess we won't be having any community picnics any time soon."

"No, I think not."

"Where the hell did those things come from? I heard they weren't from that zoo. What were they again?"

"They're calling them bear-dogs." Abe didn't say anything about Ronnie Blight claiming they had run off and left the county. No point in being a rumors monger.

"I hear there's so many funerals the mayor decided it would be best to hold a memorial to honor everyone killed that day. A candlelight vigil."

"That's right."

Abe heard yelling. He turned and saw the three teenage boys that had been playing toss with the Frisbee, racing across the campground like their lives depended on it. One of them was shouting, "Everybody, look out. It's a stampede."

"What are they yelling about?" Bron stepped away from the dumpster to get a better look at what they were running away from.

Abe rested his hand on the grip of his revolver.

Twenty mule deer came charging out of the trees. Each one weighing three hundred pounds. Half a dozen bucks with eight-point antlers, leading the herd through the campground. They were an unstoppable force.

The frantic deer plowed through the tents, some stumbling but staying on their feet. Everyone scattered to get out of their path. The ones at the picnic tables hunkered behind the concrete benches for safety. A woman tried to dodge out of the way and was knocked off her feet by a large doe, miraculously managing to crawl out of the path of the heavy hooves. A man coming out of his tent wasn't so lucky. He was gored in the shoulder by a passing buck, dragged ten feet before slipping off the horns.

Two mule deer veered, crashing into a tent trailer, and knocked it over.

Abe watched the black-tailed rumps leap between the trees as the herd vanished into the forest.

A few campers were running over to the injured man holding his bloody shoulder and assisting anyone that might have been hurt from the sudden melee.

"We're going to need some medical attention up here," Bron said.

"I'll call for an ambulance." Abe started for his cruiser.

"There are only two things that will make mule deer run like that."

Abe stopped and faced Bron. "What's that?"

"Wildfire or a very large predator."

Abe gazed into the trees where the herd had appeared. "I don't smell any smoke, do you?"

"No, I don't."

"Ah, shit."

Everyone in the campground stopped what they were doing and turned with worried looks to what sounded like a bulldozer tearing through the forest and smashing down trees, only there wasn't the rumbling of a diesel engine or the clamor of heavy machinery.

"What the hell is that?" a man yelled.

"Oh my God," a woman screamed when the mammoth bear came out of the woods.

It had long brown fur and was as wide as a transit bus with a monstrous head and paws the size of manhole covers with deadly 12-inch long claws. The sixteen-foot tall carnivore stood on its hind legs and roared. White spittle spewed out its savage mouth.

Abe had seen a photograph of this creature on TV. It was a Bergman's bear, the one that had escaped from the zoo and was reported to weigh over 4,000 pounds. It looked like a giant grizzly on steroids and was twice the size of a polar bear.

Abe drew his revolver and fired at the animal. He was a crack shot and knew he'd hit the massive bear but the creature didn't flinch. It took one look at Abe and came at him.

Knowing he had only seconds before the fierce bear mauled him, Abe turned and ran for his cruiser. He swung open the door and dove onto the front seat.

Thundering across the campground on all fours, the bear bounced up and came down on the hood of the squad car with its front paws. The metal buckled under the powerful force of the bear's weight. Coming around to the side of the vehicle, the bear smashed the roof, breaking the emergency lights.

Abe wanted desperately to close the driver's-side door. He cringed as the headliner caved-in. It was like being trapped in a car being crushed in an auto wrecker's compactor. He could feel the car tilting. The damn bear was picking up the cruiser, flipping it onto its side.

He slid against the front seat with his head and shoulders pressed up against the armrest of the passenger door. The driver-side door was wrenched off its hinges.

Glancing out the cracked windshield, Abe saw the door fly the length of a campsite and land in the dirt.

The bear looked down through the opening. Thick drool dripped down on Abe's face. A giant paw reached down...

The park ranger utility truck rammed into the bear and scooped it off its feet like a speed rusher tackling a quarterback. The two-ton creature toppled over the vehicle, crumbling the fenders and tailgate before crashing to the ground.

Any other animal would have been dead, but not Bergman's bear.

The beast was indestructible.

Rather than take its rage out on the vehicle that had just struck it, the brutish cryptid chose to annihilate the campground. It began with the nearest family-sized tent.

Bron leaped out of the utility truck. He ran over to the demolished cruiser and stepped up on the undercarriage to peer inside the car. "Are you okay?"

Abe scooted around in the seat and raised his hand. "Help me out." He pushed with his boots, letting Bron haul him up so he could climb out of the car.

There wasn't much they could do but watch helplessly as the gargantuan carnivore went berserk.

Campers scurried in every direction. The bear stormed through the campsites, trampling tents, people trapped inside screaming. It caught up to a man, crushing him to the ground.

The bear swung its right arm, slicing another man's head from his shoulders with one swipe of its sharp claws.

It poked its head into a large tent; backed out with a limp man dangling from its jaws. The bear meshed its teeth together, chomping its victim in two.

The driver of a recreation vehicle tried to pull out of a campsite, ripping the electrical cord from the receptacle on the aluminum siding. He made the mistake of taking the turn too sharply onto the paved road and flipped over.

People raced to their cars and trucks for safety.

The bear collided into automobiles pulling out to escape, forcing some to crash into trees or other cars. It continued its rampage, flattening tents, and wrecking vehicles.

Then, as if satisfying a primeval need, the beast roared and lumbered into the forest.

The campground looked like a machete-wielding psychopath had gone around hacking up campers. Abe counted seven not moving, at least twenty injured on the ground. "This is why Bergman's bear is Level-5 on the Cryptid Warning System."

"People see this, they're going to want to make this damn thing a Level-10," Bron said, shaking his head.

23

BLOOD SUCKERS

Clare sat outside in her chair beside the camper truck and reviewed her emails on her cell phone, looking for prospective customers throwing work her way. Abe had sent her an image of the Rocklin Falls Cinema with the single word CLOSED in large plastic letters on the marquee over the theater entrance. He also wrote her a short note, describing the horrible attack at the Blue Ridge campground but didn't attach any pictures. He assured her that he was unhurt but the gargantuan bear had demolished his cruiser.

She scolded herself for forgetting to recharge her cell phone before leaving home, as her battery was low. She decided to save what power she had and put the device in her coat pocket. It was bad enough the service signal was spotty back in the hills.

She looked up and watched Rounder making a perimeter sweep of the herd of goats, bunching them up as dusk approached. Her band of insatiable employees had done an excellent job of eradicating unwanted foliage for one day. Figuring the eighty 100-pound goats consumed twenty-five percent equivalent of their body weight, they had cleared away 2,000 pounds of toxic weeds and thorny bushes.

Her fat-belly maintenance crew would be sleeping well tonight.

Besides Rounder, there were ten rams to protect the herd. The dominant ram had not been determined as the Pyrenees was the alpha and could easily overpower the smaller animals whenever they became aggressive.

Clare had finished dinner: chili out of the can with two slices of homemade bread, a sliver of Myrtle's goat cheese, and a cup of coffee. Nothing fancy.

Growing up as a pole bean ragamuffin on a farm, she'd learned discipline, cutting back when times were lean, enjoying the bountiful when it came her way. She and Abe had known hardship when they were young. Clare never knew when her father would have a bumper crop to put food on the table. Abe had been a scrappy adolescent and was always fighting to stay out of street gangs before his single mom sent him to live with his grandfather on a struggling ranch just out of Rocklin Falls forty years ago.

The sun disappeared behind the distant hillside like a magnificent copper penny slipping into a coin slot.

Clare chose to leave her rifle leaning up against the side of the truck, as it was too difficult sighting a target through the scope at night. She went over, opened the gate, and went into the meadow. She had set up four battery-operated lanterns on each corner of the perimeter surrounding the goat herd. That way there would be better lighting for her to watch her animals instead of sitting with a lantern by her chair, which would have prevented her from seeing very far into the night.

She made a full-circle, switching on the lanterns. Instead of going back to wait by the truck, Clare decided to sit on a large rock not too far away from where Rounder was poised flat on his belly in a lie down position ready to burst into action at the first provocation of a predator or respond to Clare's command.

Using the light from the nearest lamp, she drew the Ruger revolver that had been handed down to her by her father after he passed. She rolled out the cylinder and checked the chamber for six cartridges. Something she often saw cowboys do in westerns before a shootout, which always made her laugh. What fool goes around with an unloaded gun?

Then why was she doing it? Nerves?

She holstered the gun, making sure the bottom of her coat didn't cover the handgrip, hindering her draw.

After fifteen minutes of sitting on the cold rock, she stood and glanced around.

She hadn't realized how dark it had become. The moon—if there was one—was shrouded by a bank of ominous clouds blanketing out the stars. The lanterns illuminated the four corners like tiny lighthouses, marking their locations but casting a limited glow.

A slight breeze chilled the air carrying a scent that caused the goats to shuffle and crowd together.

Clare looked over at the Pyrenean Mountain Dog. "On your feet."

Rounder obeyed and got up but knew not to move.

Clare felt the leather of her holster. She kept her hand poised, ready to draw and pull back the hammer in one fluid motion, squeezing the trigger and firing from the hip to hit the mark; a fast-draw technique she'd learned from her father.

Something skittered across the meadow in the dark behind her. Whatever it was, it knew to stay away from the light of the lanterns. Clare cocked her head trying to hear above the restless goats. She heard movement to her right then fast footfalls racing to the left. Judging from what she heard, the predators were not four-legged.

These things were running on two feet.

The herd suddenly scattered in all directions, some goats wailing.

Clare yelled, "Away," and Rounder charged into the herd. She drew her gun and held it at her side with the muzzle pointed down. She stood her ground like a boulder in the middle of a swift-moving stream, forcing the frightened goats to veer around her.

Rounder let out a series of sharp barks then bolted through the frantic flock.

Clare caught sight of a predator stepping into the light.

The hideous creature stood four feet tall on its hind legs. The thing looked like a giant hairless rat. It had an egg-shaped head, grotesque face with fish eyes, and a gaping mouth that looked like a bowl, rimmed with pointy needle-sharp teeth—which at the moment were dripping blood.

The neck was taut; its shoulders hunched. Bony knobs ran down its spine ending at the base of the tailbone to the two-foot long serpentine tail.

At the end of each arm was a two-claw appendage; three-talon toes on its hind feet.

Clare had never seen a live creature before but she knew what it was as she'd read about them and watched news reports on the television after the zoo tragedy.

The chupacabra hissed at the lantern and vanished out of the light.

A panicked goat blatted, its cry echoed by the other livestock.

As more of the flock cut around her, Clare could see silhouettes in front of the backdrop of light, hunched over the fallen goats. She ran over, grabbed a lantern, and marched toward the malevolent figures with her gun pointed.

Two chupacabras knelt over the same goat, feeding on its blood.

Clare raised the revolver...

Rounder plowed into the two bloodsuckers, smashing them to the ground. They immediately skittered to their feet to escape. The big dog pounced on the nearest creature, shoving it back to the ground with its powerful front paws. The chupacabra hissed then screeched when Rounder sunk his fangs into the back of its neck, severing its spine. The creature clawed at the dirt and went still.

The chupacabras were like specters weaving between the goats. Each time Clare got a bead on one, it would dash off to feed on another goat. Rounder gave chase every chance he got but the quick-footed monsters were too fast for him.

Clare heard footsteps coming up behind her. She spun around.

A chupacabra leaped at her from out of the darkness. Her gun flew from her hand as she slammed onto her back. She raised her left forearm to protect her face. The grotesque creature bit into her coat sleeve. Its pointy teeth punctured the fabric and dug deep into her flesh to the bone.

"Get the hell off of me." Clare swung her right hand and punched the ugly thing in the side of the head. It teetered to one side as if it were going to fall over then righted itself. The chupacabra clawed her face, slicing through her cheek. She raised her hips trying to buck it off but it clung on. Her right hand felt around the ground until her fingers touched the handgrip of her revolver.

The large-caliber bullet punched a hole in the chupacabra's forehead, shattering the back of its skull. Bone chips and bloody gore rained down onto Clare's face and clothes.

She pushed the dead creature off. She got to her feet. She wiped her face with her sleeve. Pissed as hell, she trudged through the field, catching glimpses and firing her gun.

She tripped, her knees coming down on a dead goat. Clare got up. She spotted a fleeing figure and shot at it.

The herd had congregated by the gate.

Clare picked up a lantern and held it high above her head. She counted ten goats dead on the ground.

Rounder bounded up to her side.

Clare laid her hand on his head and looked into his face. "That'll do."

The dog understood; his work was done; at least for now.

It was important she get immediate medical attention. Even though the bite wasn't life threatening at the moment, she worried about getting a bacterial infection. For all she knew, the damn things were rabid. She reached inside her coat pocket and took out her cell phone. Luckily, she had a signal.

Abe answered on the second ring.

24

OUT OF THE ASHES

Toby downshifted the Barracuda, turned, and headed down the dirt road toward the nursery. The convertible top was down so he drove slowly so as not to kick up too much dust. He turned to Alice in the front passenger seat. "I hope I didn't scare you back there."

"No, not at all," Alice replied, unclenching her fingers from the armrest. She was glad she had worn a scarf on her head or her fine hair would have been a tangled mess from the windy ride.

The parking lot was empty when they pulled up to the nursery entrance. Toby turned off the throaty engine. "That's odd. The gate's closed."

Alice checked her wristwatch. "Laney should have opened an hour ago."

"I wonder what..." Toby glanced around, sniffing the air. "Do you smell that?"

Alice took a whiff. "Smells like there's been a fire."

Toby looked at Alice. "You don't think their place burned down?"

"Oh God, should we call someone?"

"No, not until we're sure." Toby got out. He walked around the front of the car. He opened Alice's door.

"Aren't you the gentleman."

"Chivalry might be dead but I'm not." He helped her out. "Let's go this way." Toby led Alice to the corner of the cyclone fence. "Be careful, it's a little rocky."

"Glad I wore my sensible shoes," Alice said, stepping onto the uneven ground.

Toby kept one hand on the mesh fence for support as they went along. "Do you ever wonder if Laney's husband might be involved in something shady?"

"What do you mean?"

"I don't know, maybe he's under investigation? Would explain that black Expedition I spotted following me."

"You mean the one you think parks down my street?"

"Probably the FBI. For all we know it's the DEA and Allen's a big time drug dealer."

"That's absurd. Laney would never get mixed up in that sort of thing."

"Might explain why he stays secluded."

They reached the end of the fence line and walked over to a dirt trail leading into a stand of maple trees, the smell of a recent fire growing stronger the further they went.

Alice spotted a structure beyond the trees. "That must be the cottage. Thank God, it's okay." They turned left at the fork and followed the path to the back porch.

Toby knocked on the door. He gave it a few seconds and knocked again. He looked at Alice. "Doesn't look like anyone's home."

"Try the door."

"Better stand back."

"Why?"

"In case it's booby trapped."

"I seriously doubt that."

"Okay, nice knowing you." Toby turned the knob and pushed open the door. He stuck his head in. "Ah Jesus, Alice, you got to see this."

Alice followed Toby inside. She saw bullet holes in the cabinets and walls, blood smeared on the floor. "What do you think happened?"

"Someone must have busted in."

"I hope they're okay."

"Stay here. I'll check the rest of the house."

"Be careful."

Toby grabbed a carving knife from the block on the counter. He crept into the other room. He returned after canvassing the cottage. "I checked everywhere. There's no one here." He laid the knife on the kitchen table.

"Maybe they're at the greenhouse."

They went outside to the fork in the trail and followed the other path until they reached an enormous charred heap of smoldering rubble. Smoky tendrils rose out of the melted glass and black ash.

"This wasn't an accident," Toby said. "This place was torched. You can smell the accelerant."

"Why would someone do this?"

"Looks like someone was trying to put Allen out of business."

"You don't think Laney and her husband were inside?"

"I'd say there's a good—" Toby paused when something stirred in the ruins.

"Toby, what's that?" Alice pointed to an oval shape protruding out of the charred debris. She watched the thing push slowly out of the ground, first a head, then the shoulders and torso. She gasped as the blackened life form continued to sprout and finally broke through the desiccated soil.

It looked like a man covered in soot.

"No way," Toby said. "No damn way."

"Hose," the charred man said. He took a step forward and fell to his knees. "Hurry," he pleaded.

Alice turned and saw a faucet bib a few feet away with a garden hose attached. "Toby, he wants us to wash him off."

Toby grabbed the spray nozzle and dragged the hose behind him. He pulled the trigger. A steady spray hit the man in the face and chest. He got to his feet so Toby could completely rinse down his body.

After all the soot was washed off, Alice was shocked to see the man was naked and his skin wasn't flesh tone but looked more like the rind of a green lime.

"Thank you," the strange man said. "I was suffocating there."

"What are...who are you?" Toby asked.

"I'm Allen Moss."

"Oh, my God. You're Laney's husband?"

"That's right."

"How in the world did you survive the fire?" Alice asked.

"I rooted myself into the ground. Not exactly a fun thing, believe me."

Alice and Toby exchanged puzzled looks.

"I know it's a lot to wrap your heads around. Anyway, thanks Toby."

"You know my name?"

"I know all of my customers' names, Toby Mack. And you're Alice Kendrick."

"That's right, but how do you know? We've never met."

"The cure-all herbs in your bodies give off a pheromone."

Toby put his hand to his nose. "All I smell is Old Spice."

"Where's Laney?" Alice asked.

"They took her."

"Who did?"

"Men working for Wilde Enterprises."

"You mean she was kidnapped?" Toby asked.

"That's right."

"I've heard that name before," Alice said. "When I was leaving my doctor visit, I overheard him on the phone, speaking to someone at Wilde Pharmaceuticals."

"Those guys," Toby snarled. "Most of my medication was by those crooks."

"Is that why they burned down your greenhouse? To get rid of the competition?" Alice asked.

"No. It was to pay us back for destroying Wilde property."

"What will become of Laney?"

"I don't know but it won't be good. I'm going to need your help."

Alice looked at Toby. He nodded his head. She turned back to Allen. "Tell us what to do."

"I'm going to need a ride."

"Okay," Alice said. "Let's go to the cottage and get you some clothes."

"I'm sorry, but there aren't any."

"Oh?"

"I got a sweatshirt and some gym stuff in my trunk you could wear," Toby offered.

Alice asked, "But how will we find her?"

"By the scent from the bracelet she is wearing," Allen said.

"So what are we waiting for? Let's go get Laney."

25

NIGHT TERRORS

Nick hadn't expected they would be stuck in so much traffic. Barriers had been set up blocking a major exit onto a main highway, causing the congestion. He could have gotten out of the car and covered the distance they had traveled in the past half-hour in five minutes on foot.

Luckily, their turnoff was coming up. He checked his watch. He figured another twenty minutes until they were there, and after check-in, they might have less than half an hour to spend with Gabe before they would be asked to leave.

Thirty agonizing minutes later, Meg gazed out her window at the gardeners jockeying lawn mowers and trimming hedges of the lush green landscaping canvassing each side of the driveway leading up to Brentwood Meadows. "Nice to see our therapy dollars at work."

Nick turned into the lot. He parked in a vacant stall by the psychiatric institute's front entrance.

They hurried inside.

Once they had checked in at the receptionist desk, and gotten their visitor passes, they waited to be buzzed in through the security door. Nick hated the smell. It always reeked of unwashed bodies and soiled sanitary diapers. There wasn't enough Pine Sol in the world to mask the putrid odor. He often wondered if it was the rotting of all those damaged brains stinking up the place—such a terrible waste.

A nurse by the medication dispensary saw them coming down the hall. "Mr. and Mrs. Wells. It's so nice to see you."

Nick wished he could say the same. "Nurse Fleming. We were hoping to be here sooner but we got caught up in traffic."

"Before you see Gabe, Dr. Phelps would like to have a word."

"Can't it wait?" Meg protested. "I would like to see my boy."

"He assured me it would only take a minute."

Meg started to say something else but Nick silenced her by placing his hand on her arm. "The sooner we talk to the doctor, the sooner we can see our son."

Nick could tell Meg wasn't happy but what choice did they have. Nurse Fleming would just refuse to buzz them into the recreation room where Gabe was sitting with no expectation or realization his parents had come for a visit, only that it was time for a change of scenery from being cooped up in his tiny room.

An orderly in a white shirt and pants—a gorilla that probably worked part-time as a bouncer in a strip club—escorted Nick and Meg down the hall to the doctor's office.

The door was open. Dr. Phelps looked up from an open file. "Nick, Meg, come in." He motioned for them to have a seat in the two chairs in front of his desk.

After they sat down, Meg asked, "Please tell us you have good news."

"Well, I don't think it's totally bad."

Nick loathed the man's bedside manner. "I thought Gabe was making progress."

"He is. But not like we had hoped. I know I've asked this countless times before, but what did happen to your son?"

"That's the thing. We have no idea. He never spoke about it. He just slipped into this fugue." Nick looked at Meg. She gave him a blank stare and nodded.

"As we haven't been able to get a word out of him, I've taken a new tactic and had a camera set up in his room."

"What? Why?" It was bad enough Gabe had to be here, now they were violating his privacy? Nick could feel his blood boiling.

"I believe the root of his problems are the night terrors."

Meg leaned forward in her seat. "He's experiencing nightmares?"

"Yes."

"Why weren't we told of this?"

"We weren't aware until a night nurse heard him screaming and found him thrashing about in his bed. He was doing fine under moderate sedation for all this time but now it seems he's having increasing bouts of violent episodes during his sleep. We were forced to move him down to a room at the end of the hall so he doesn't disturb the other patients."

Nick was about to lose it. "Oh, heaven forbid, we disturb the cuckoo's nest."

"Honey, please." It was Meg's turn to be the rational one.

Dr. Phelps clasped his hands together on the desk. "We've also had to restrain him at night for his own protection."

"My son's not crazy. He just needs help." *Next you'll be suggesting Gabe undergo electrical shock treatment*, Nick almost blurted.

"And we're giving it to him. Your son does talk in his sleep. The only problem is we haven't been able to decipher what he is saying. It's almost like he is talking in tongues."

"Like that religious thing?" Meg said.

"Yes. It's important that we don't rush things. I would hate for him to have a psychotic break."

Nick turned and saw Meg's eyes tear up. He took a breath, then looked at the doctor. "Can we see our son?"

"As you wish." Dr. Phelps stood. He waved the orderly in from the hallway. "Please take Mr. and Mrs. Wells to the recreation room."

"Yes, sir. Will you please come with me?" the orderly asked Nick and Meg.

As they walked down the hall, Nick glanced through the double-pane glass window at his son sitting alone inside the recreation room. The teenager, who had once been energetic and full of life, challenging at times but always Nick's pride and joy, was now despondent and listless; a catatonic lost soul. Gabe looked like he hadn't showered or changed his hospital pajamas in days, his hair a tangled bird nest. Surely they could have cleaned him up for the visit.

The orderly unlocked the door. Nick draped his arm around Meg's shoulder and gave her a hug. She looked at him, forcing a smile.

They entered the room.

* * *

The haunting nightmare is always the same...

"Get up Gabe. We're going out!"

Gabe opens his eyes after drifting off watching television. "What time is it?"

"Hell, I don't know," Shane says. "Let's go and explore."

Gabe sits up, swings his legs off the bed. He rubs his eyes. "We can't go out there. It's two in the morning."

"What? Mommy won't let you?"

"Shut up, Shane."

"Pussy."

"All right, I'll go. Quit being a jerk."

"Well, looky here. Gabe just found his balls."

"Screw you."

"Touché brother."

Wearing hooded sweatshirts, they sneak out of the room. They creep down the rear stairwell to the ground floor exit door so the hotel staff won't see them and slip outside into the dark. There are no stars, no night sky; just the underbelly structure of the dome roof 25 stories above their heads covering Cryptid Zoo.

"Where are we going?" Gabe always asks Shane.

"To Sea Monster Cove."

"Again?"

"That's right. And we'll keep going until you admit that sea serpent is a fake."

"Looks real to me."

"No!" Shane says. "I'm telling you it's nothing but a mechanical sea serpent on a track like the Jaws shark that attacks the ride at Universal Studios. I'll prove it."

They pass the sign marking the entrance to the attraction. They go down the concrete steps between the bleachers until they reach the water's edge. The cadborosaurus' back is visible on the surface as it swims underwater around the small island.

Shane points, saying too loudly, "See, it's nothing but pumps and—"

The sea serpent lunges out of the water.

Shane scampers up the concrete steps.

Gabe narrowly misses being eaten and races up to the top of the bleachers. "Think it's fake now?"

"Big deal, so it's real."

And then Gabe sees the globster, Patrick; the hideous blob the size of a beanbag chair. The mysterious undead carcass is slimy and gray with two-deep socket eyeholes and a puckered mouth. It drags itself toward Shane with its two stubbly arms and webbed hands.

"There's no way that's real." Shane grabs a gaff leaning against a wall. He drives the barbed spear deep into the thing. He pulls out the shaft dripping with jelly-like slime and tosses the gaff onto the platform.

Patrick keeps advancing.

"You better watch out," Gabe warns.

"Why, you think it's going to eat me?" Shane squats. He waves his hand, taunting the creeping blob. Showing off, he grins at Gabe.

The globster lunges, takes Shane's entire arm into its mouth.

"Holy shit!" Shane yells.

Gabe rushes over, pulls Shane back, freeing his arm.

Shane takes one look at the oozing shriveling appendage with webbed nubs for fingers on his wilted hand and screams.

They return to the room. Gabe worries Shane's whimpering will wake up Shane's parents in the adjoining suite. "Shut up," he hisses.

Shane slides into bed and crawls under the covers. Gabe sees wet patches bloom on the absorbent fabric.

"Gabe, help me..."

"Shut up! This is all your fault."

The shriveled hand extends out from under the blanket. "Gabe, pleaassssseeeee..."

* * *

Gabe snapped awake, drenched with sweat.

Lying flat on the mattress, he couldn't feel his hands confined in the leather restraints. His ankles were numb as well from being bound to the foot of the bed.

The room was dark except for a patch of light shining in through the door's small observation window from the dimly lit hallway.

He rolled his head to the side. He looked down. The top sheet had slipped off and was on the floor.

He glanced up at the camera positioned in the corner of the ceiling. He wondered if the night nurse was watching him right now, if she would come in and cover him up.

He was so cold.

Gabe raised his head. He looked down at the grotesque jellyfish blob where his body should be.

He screamed.

And kept screaming.

* * *

"Gabe, calm down. There's nothing to be afraid of," the night nurse said, leaning over him.

But he couldn't stop blabbering.

Make it stop!

Pleaassssseeee make it stop!

26

INMATES

When Jack woke up, he had no idea where he was, only that he was lying on his side on a concrete floor inside a large jail cell.

And he wasn't alone.

He could hear heavy breathing behind him. It sounded like a large animal; a very large animal. He reached back and his fingers touched a thick matt of hair.

Jack sat up slowly and turned.

He recognized the orangey coat on the extended leg. "Thank God, I thought they'd shot you with real bullets."

Lennie sat with his back against the concrete wall. He had a dopey expression on his face from the high-dosage sedative tranquilizer darts still sticking in his chest. The yeren gave Jack a lopsided grin, drooling like a dental patient numbed with too much Novocain. Knowing Lennie was too out of it to feel anything, Jack plucked the darts from the Chinese ape-man's chest.

"I'm going to scope things out while you get your bearings." Jack stood and glanced around. The jail cell was really an animal enclosure. He estimated the containment to be a twenty-foot square box with an equally high ceiling with three concrete walls. The fourth side had two-inch thick steel bars facing out to another giant cage on the other side of a walkway.

The last thing Jack remembered before passing out after crashing the van was Nora unconscious on the passenger seat and Lennie being subdued.

So where was Nora? Had she died in the accident? Jack felt a sickly pang in his stomach. Like a liposuction machine had suddenly pumped it dry.

He heard footsteps coming down the walkway. He went over and gripped the bars. He was shocked to see Dr. Joel McCabe approaching. The doctor looked disheveled as always wearing his customary lab coat, this one splotched with blood.

"Well, look who we have here," Dr. McCabe said, grinning at Jack.

"Aren't you supposed to be in prison?"

"So I am."

"This is insane. Where's Nora? Is she okay?"

"Couldn't tell you. Better ask him." McCabe turned.

Ivan Connors walked up and stood beside the geneticist. A keycard badge was clipped to his shirt pocket. "I assure you, she's alive and well."

"I want to see her."

"Sorry, no can do. She's not here."

"Where is she?"

"I'm afraid that's no longer any of your concern."

"You do know what they do to kidnappers."

Dr. McCabe broke into laughter. "Yeah, they throw them in prison." The doctor threw up his arms. In doing so, his right hand swept in front of Connors' shirt. "Guess what—we're already here."

Jack noticed the keycard badge was no longer clipped to Connors' pocket. Rather than mention it, he said, "What do you mean, we're already here?"

"You're in Stoneham Correctional Facility," Connors said.

McCabe turned slightly so Connors couldn't see the doctor's hands behind his back holding a blue device with a handgrip to the keycard. It was a Radio-Frequency Identification card reader. McCabe was copying the information on the badge onto the electronic device.

Not knowing what the doctor was up to, but thinking he better play along, Jack decided not to alert Connors and said, "The prison?"

"One and the same."

"So what are we doing here?"

Connors gave Jack a lecherous Joker grin. "I hear the food is great here. The company, not so much."

Jack glared at Connors. "You're putting me in with a bunch of convicts?"

"That's right."

"You can't do that."

"Sure I can. Carter Wilde owns this prison."

"And what happens to Lennie?"

"I'm afraid that's up to Dr. McCabe."

"You better not hurt him. Let us out, right now."

"Sorry, Tremens, not going to happen." Connors glanced at his wristwatch. "Enjoy your stay."

"You can't do this," Jack said, gripping the bars so hard his knuckles turned white.

Connors looked down and noticed his keycard was gone. "What the..."

"Looking for that?" Dr. McCabe pointed to the badge on the floor behind Connors' right boot.

Connors bent down, picked up the keycard, and clipped it back on his shirt pocket. He headed off down the walkway and was soon out of sight.

Dr. McCabe transferred the data from the RFID reader onto a master clone card.

"What are you planning to do with that?" Jack asked.

"This Jack Tremens, is my Get Out of Jail Free card."

27

COOTIES

Abe leaned on the metal fence railing and watched Clare's goats march single file down the chute into the chemical solution. The passage was narrow so the animals couldn't balk and try to turn around. The livestock entering one by one became completely submerged then surfaced, swimming out of the dipping tank. Once out of the bath they shook off and trotted up the ramp into a holding pen.

"Thanks for doing this," Abe said to Daren Sikes, the local rancher who had offered to disinfect the goats that had come in contact with the mite-infested chupacabras.

"Parasites aren't to be trifled with. I suggest if you aren't going to shave them, we better run them through again for a double-dip."

"Sure. What about Rounder? Don't tell me we're going to have to shave him."

"Him I would. I can make a call and have someone over here within the hour. She normally shears sheep. I'm sure his hair would grow back fairly fast."

"If you think that's best."

"I've seen what mites can do, especially to the face and ears, and I have to say it isn't pretty. Damn things get under the skin; you've got one sick animal."

"If it's okay with you, I need to get to the hospital."

"Sure thing, Sheriff. If you like, once the goats have been treated and I've disinfected your trailer, I can bring them around to your place."

"I'd appreciate that."

"Give my best to Clare."

"I will, Daren. And thanks again."

"No problem, Sheriff."

* * *

Abe parked his Bronco—his cruiser being a total wreck—at the curb outside the hospital's front entrance. He went inside, passed through the lobby, and took the elevator to the third floor.

He gave the nurse sitting at her station a friendly nod then headed down the corridor to Clare's room. He opened the door.

"Safe to come in?" he asked.

"If you're not afraid of catching cooties."

Abe stepped in the room.

Clare was sitting up in her bed. She was wearing a powder blue hospital gown. Her left forearm was bandaged. Her red-toned face and exposed skin looked like it had been scrubbed raw with a scouring pad.

"I brought you a change of clothes." Abe held up a plastic bag. He opened the little closet and looked inside. "Where are the clothes you were wearing?"

"The orderly took them down to the incinerator and burned them."

"What, they couldn't be washed?"

"Not if you saw what was crawling in them. Believe me, there was no way I'd ever wear them again."

"How are you feeling?"

"Like I'm being eaten alive. Damn things have burrowed under my skin. The doctor says it's the worst case of scabies he's ever seen. I hope you burned those chupacabras."

"The owner of the property took care of it. What about your arm?"

"They cleaned the bite and put me on antibiotics."

"No threat of rabies?"

"There was enough brain matter on my clothes for them to run a test. It came out negative."

"Thank God."

"How's Rounder?"

"He's undergoing what you might call a bit of a makeover. Let's say he's going to look a lot slimmer the next time you see him."

"Make sure the vet takes a look at him."

"I will."

"How many goats did we lose?"

"Eleven."

Tears streaked down Clare's cheeks. Abe took a step toward the bed.

"Sorry, Abe, but I don't think a hug would be advisable."

"Oh, yeah, I forgot. Cooties."

28

THE LITTER

Miguel followed Maria down the hallway. He had a bundle of old towels in his arms. “Shouldn’t we be boiling water or something?”

“Very funny,” Maria said. She opened the door to the spare bedroom reserved for whenever they had guests but had been converted into a temporary birthing den for Rosie. Miguel had formed a cardboard enclosure large enough for the black Labrador to sprawl comfortably when nursing her pups. The area was covered with sheets of newspaper.

At the moment, Rosie was resting on a throw rug next to her bowls of water and food.

Miguel placed the towels on the floor in the corner of the room. He knelt beside Rosie and scratched behind her ear. “Better put on a good show girl. Sophia’s pretty excited.”

Maria grabbed the towel off the top of the bundle. She shook it out and laid the towel flat in the makeshift delivery den. “This will be the first time Sophia’s seen a birth before.”

“Hope she doesn’t freak out.”

“It will be good for her. To see a new life come into the world.”

Sophia had a worried look on her face as she entered the room.

“What’s wrong sweetie?” Maria asked.

“Rosie won’t eat.”

“That’s because she’s about to have her pups. It’s perfectly natural.”

Miguel looked at Maria. “Should we prepare her?”

“For what, Papa?” Sophia asked.

“Come sit on the bed.” Maria sat down on the mattress and patted the comforter. Sophia sat beside her mother. The little girl looked up like a child eager to hear a favorite bedtime story.

Before Maria began, Miguel coaxed Rosie onto her feet. He ushered her inside the area blocked off with cardboard. Rosie circled, clawing the floor and shredded the sheets of newspaper, before finally flopping down onto her side.

“Tell me, Mama,” Sophia insisted.

“Well, when the pups come out, they’ll be inside clear sacks.”

"Like lunch bags you put my sandwiches in?"

"Not exactly. More of a membrane."

"What's a mem brain?"

Miguel fought to keep a straight face.

Maria saw him stifling a laugh and mouthed the words, "Shut up."

"It protects the puppies when they're inside Rosie," Miguel said, hoping to clarify.

"Anyway," Maria continued, "when each puppy comes out, Rosie will have to bite through the membrane and lick it off so she can clean them."

"Did you have to do that with me when I was born, Mama?"

Miguel couldn't help himself and broke out laughing.

"No, Sophia. Mama didn't have to do that," Maria said.

Rosie growled. She was glaring at the curtain covering the bedroom window. She began to bark.

"What is it girl?" Miguel said.

Something crashed against the glass.

"Miguel?" Maria put her arm around Sophia.

"I'll go take a look." Miguel rushed out of the room. He raced down the hall into the kitchen. He reached up, took down the shotgun, and fed two cartridges from his pocket into the chamber.

Stepping outside, he closed the backdoor behind him. It sounded like a large bird flapping its wings on the side of the house. He edged around the corner.

A gray mothman hovered outside Sophia's bedroom window. It had a six-foot wingspan and three-talon claws on the front of each wing much like a bat though it resembled a giant owl. It had a small rounded head and a short body with gangly legs that bent at the knees like a human's and four-toed feet.

Oddly, the creature had no beak or any nasal passages. The mouth was open in the shape of a big O. The mostly alarming features were its eyes, which glowed bright red.

Miguel averted staring directly at the mothman. As exhibits at Cryptid Zoo, he knew the creatures possessed a strange ability of foreseeing the future and could implant the same hypnotic vision into a person's mind merely by looking into their eyes.

The mothman swooped towards him. Before he could raise the shotgun barrel, the creature gripped him by the shirt with its sharp talons. It lowered its head and gazed into Miguel's eyes. Miguel felt a strange sensation like his brain was expanding behind his eyeballs...

"Mama, Rosie's first puppy is coming out." Sophia is ecstatic. The black Labrador pants. Out of the dog's birth canal and onto the

shredded newspaper comes a yellowish blob, something straight out of a nightmare. Sophia screams. Instead of a cute whelp, the thing is a hideous eyeless abomination of wrinkled flesh and needlepoint teeth. Blood gushes out of Rosie. The thing crawls toward the cardboard wall, rises on its hind legs. The grotesque creature leaps on Sophia...

Miguel shook his head to clear his mind. He brandished the shotgun like a club and struck the mothman, dislodging its talons from his shirt. Before he could get off a shot, the creature flew into the trees.

Sophia screamed inside the house.

"Jesus." Miguel sprinted down the side yard. He raced to the backdoor and bolted inside the house.

Sophia continued to scream.

Miguel charged down the hallway to the spare room. Maria and Sophia were sitting on the edge of the bed. Maria had her arm around their daughter.

"What happened?" he asked, catching his breath.

"Papa look," Sophia said, pointing into the cardboard enclosure. "There's something wrong with Rosie's puppies."

Miguel stepped toward the birthing area and saw Rosie had already given birth to two pups.

Sophia began to cry. "They're different."

"It's okay sweetie," Maria said. She looked up at Miguel. "She doesn't understand why the puppies aren't black like Rosie."

Miguel looked down at the yellow pups. "That's because Gunther's their father."

29

AFFINITY

Nora blinked at the harsh light as the blindfold was removed.

Red floor numbers flashed on the digital screen. Nora felt a hollow sensation in the pit of her stomach as the freight elevator raced upward. Ivan Connors stood by her side in the spacious lift, watching her like a mongrel guarding its food dish.

Nora brushed her hair from her face, her fingers touching the bandage on her forehead. She looked down and saw a small smudge of blood on her fingertips.

She turned her attention back to the floor counter. They had passed 145 and were still rocketing up. She looked at Connors. "Where are you taking me?"

Connors continued his stone-cold stare.

The elevator finally shuddered to a stop. Nora gawked at the digital display. "Wait a minute, that can't be right. We're on the 183rd floor?"

"That's right." Connors inserted a key into a slot on the control panel. The elevator doors opened. He escorted Nora down a hallway, turning left at a corridor.

Connors stopped at a door. He inserted a keycard into a reader below the door handle. A green light came on. He pulled down the handle and opened the door. He shoved Nora into the dimly lit room, locking her inside.

She waited a moment to allow her eyes to adjust to the darkness. She expected to see a bunk or a washbasin, a lidless toilet in the corner: the bare necessities of a jail cell.

Instead, she saw a mostly vacated triangular room with crates scattered about the floor.

Nora heard a noise coming from behind a crate. "Who's there?"

A woman stood. She studied Nora for a moment. "Hey, don't I know you?"

"I don't think so," Nora replied, though the woman did look vaguely familiar.

"I know where. It was on Miguel's computer. You guys were doing one of those face chat things."

"Now I remember. You were in that bar in Madagascar, sitting at Jack and Miguel's table."

"That would be me."

"I thought you were the waitress."

"Hardly. Then you must be Nora. The cryptozoologist who hired Jack and Miguel."

"That's right. And you are?"

"I'm Laney. Laney Moss."

"Oh my God. You're Allen Moss's wife? We thought you both died on the island."

"No, we managed to escape."

"So what are you doing here?"

"Connors' men."

"They kidnapped you?"

"That's right."

"Where's Allen?"

Laney hung her head. "He's dead."

"Oh, Laney. I'm so sorry."

"They finally caught up to us. They killed him; payback for Allen destroying Wilde's equipment in the Amazon."

"Jack and I have been on the run as well."

"Why, what did you do?"

"We stole one of his cryptids."

"So where's Jack?"

"I wish I knew."

"So now we're what, prisoners?"

"Looks that way. Do you have any idea where we are?" Nora asked.

"No. I was blindfolded when I was brought here."

"Same here. Look around. Maybe we can figure a way out of here." Nora stepped between the unmarked crates. The bottoms of her shoes scraped across the floor. She looked down at her feet and was surprised to see a rough surface concrete still in a construction phase which needed to be smoothed over with a float trowel.

Laney paced the inside perimeter. "This is weird."

"What is?" Nora asked.

"The walls. They're all made of glass." Laney pressed her nose against the opaque glass, cupping her hands on both sides of her face. "It's dark, but I think there's another room on the other side."

Nora looked about the room. "I don't believe it."

"What is it?"

"This can't be real." Nora walked up to Laney. "We're in an animal enclosure."

"What, like in a zoo?"

"That's exactly what I mean."

A loud thump made them jump followed by an unnerving screech like fingernails on a chalkboard.

Nora and Laney turned slowly and saw a giant paw dragging its long claws down the opposite side of the glass.

30

UNLEASH THE BEASTS

Jack stared through the bars, each hand clutching a steel rod.

Ten minutes ago, two inmates had passed by carrying keycards and small black handheld tablets with plastic antennas. Dr. McCabe was up to something, setting a diabolic plan into motion.

Jack's shoulders tensed as he shook the bars. "Damn it, how the hell are we going to get out of here?" He looked over his shoulder. Lennie sat by the wall, massaging the wounds on his chest caused by the tranquilizer darts.

"Hey, big guy, get over here," Jack said, waving the yeren over.

Either Lennie was bored fussing over his injuries or he just wanted to stretch his legs. He got to his feet slowly and ambled over next to Jack.

"Grab the bars." Jack demonstrated by gripping the metal posts.

Lennie wrapped his fat fingers around the steel.

"Now, do this." Jack exaggerated by shaking his arms like he was Hercules attempting to rip the bars from the ceiling and floor.

The yeren narrowed its brow, giving him a puzzled look.

"Come on. Just do it."

A shrill emergency alarm screeched on the ceiling in the hall.

Lennie roared, shaking his head like the piercing sound was an annoying bug that had flown inside his ear. He looked up at the source of the deafening noise. He tried to reach between the bars, but his forearm was too wide to fit.

Jack wanted desperately to cover his ears but he knew if he did, he might be passing up the perfect opportunity to break out of their jail cell. He throttled the bars again. "Lennie, you can do it!"

The Chinese wildman growled. He grabbed the bars and shook them. The steel anchors broke loose. Dust and pieces of concrete rained down.

"That's it," Jack shouted. "You got it. Harder!"

Lennie yanked out the two steel poles. He tossed one, sending it clanking onto the floor. He used the other to smash the siren on the ceiling, silencing the shrill.

More alarms sounded somewhere in the building and outside.

"Good job." Jack was about to slip through the opening when he heard what sounded like a stampede charging down the hall.

Two bear-size creatures stopped in front of the jail cell. Their faces looked like Lon Chaney Jr. as the Wolfman and had white fangs and teeth on slack jaws with flop ears on the side of their enormous heads. Eyes so red, they glowed. The beasts had abundantly long, shaggy gray hair.

They wore tight-fitting shock collars equipped with GoPro cameras around their necks.

Jack remembered seeing such creatures on a cryptology classification chart hanging in Nora's office once.

Dr. McCabe had created Ozark howlers.

Judging by their collars, the doctor had devised a way to monitor their whereabouts and actions with the lightweight cameras and could control the beasts' behavior by remotely inducing electrical shocks.

The howlers snarled, stepping up to the bars.

Jack backed away. He looked up at Lennie expecting the big guy to challenge the two monsters and send them on their way but instead Jack saw something he had never seen before in the yeren's eyes—*fear*. While sharing quarters in the Biped Habitat in Cryptid Zoo, Lennie had tolerated the Bili apes in the next enclosure, and they were bat-shit-crazy—capable of attacking a full-grown lion and ripping it apart.

Making the howlers the ultimate bad asses.

Jack heard electrical *snaps* on the shock collars. The two howlers yowled and turned suddenly, bounding down the hall in the direction they were headed before stopping in front of the jail cell.

Gazing up at Lennie, Jack said, "You're going to have to remove two more if you're going to fit through." Which was like expecting a dog to recite the alphabet. He grabbed the bars again and shook them. When Lennie didn't respond, Jack stepped through the bar, turned, and gave them another shake. This time, Lennie got the gist of the command.

The yeren grabbed the next two bars by the opening, and with brute strength, wrenched them out, the steel posts narrowly missing Jack as they fell, banging on the floor.

Even with four bars missing, Lennie barely squeezed out.

Instead of turning left in the direction the howlers had taken, Jack decided they should head the other way. Running down the hall, Jack stopped at a large plate glass window facing outside. From his vantage point, Jack figured they were on the third floor of the building. High concrete walls topped with large loops of injurious razor wire surrounded three spacious areas.

Lennie gazed out the window and let out a menacing growl.

Down below, a door opened onto an exercise yard with a few picnic benches and workout areas with bench presses and barbell weights. Men in orange jumpsuits bolted from the building into the yard. They kept pouring out like a parade of army ants, some falling down and getting back up, while others became trampled as more and more frightened convicts scrambled outside.

An Ozark howler burst out of the doorway, tearing the metal door off its hinges.

Realizing there was nowhere for them to run, the men congregated with their backs against the wall. Jack figured there had to be over two hundred inmates huddled together.

Gunshots rang out inside the prison.

A prison guard charged out of the building. He leveled his riot shotgun at the giant beast.

The other howler came running out. It pounced on the guard, ripping the man apart with its teeth and claws. The attack was so savage and quick; Jack couldn't believe the scattered chunks on the ground had been a human being mere seconds ago.

The gray howlers stormed into the orange throng. It was like watching a pair of super soldiers on a manic video game, annihilating the enemy and leaving a maze of blood drenched bodies in their wake.

More prison guards rushed out. They ratcheted their weapons, popping off shots and firing into the crowd.

Inmates dropped to the ground like knocked over chess pieces.

The howlers mowed through the concourse, leaving a melee of dead bodies behind. It didn't matter how strong or tough the inmate; the howlers were merciless, vicious killing machines.

Jack looked down at another enclosure. A giant pig stood on its hind legs, rooting through a green dumpster. The thing had to be as big as a bison. A rollup door rose and the swine charged inside the building.

Glancing back, the exercise yard looked like a battlefield. No one was left standing. Bodies piled like the bloody aftermath of a fierce battle.

The howlers raced back into the building.

Jack could see a small fleet of four white trucks parked next to the prison wall.

Two trucks pulled away slowly in single file. A third truck had the back door raised, a ramp on the ground. The howlers appeared and stormed into the back of the truck. The driver shut the door. He ran up the side of the vehicle, and climbed into the cab. The three trucks drove away down a gravel road bordering a forest.

One truck had been left behind.

He slapped Lennie on the side. "We might get out of here yet."

They followed the corridor, stopping at an open door. Jack saw chairs and couches facing a large screen TV. The sound was muted. A reporter with a microphone stood by a waist-high barrier fence. The camera pulled away and panned upward to a towering skyscraper. Scrolling at the bottom of the screen were the words: WILDE SKYWAY DEDICATION CEREMONY TO CROWN THE TALLEST BUILDING IN THE WORLD.

Jack and Lennie continued down the hall until they reached Dr. McCabe's laboratory. The place was vacated. Empty filing cabinet drawers left open; the workbenches void of equipment. Jack spotted something on a desk. It was the HID reader that Dr. McCabe had used to duplicate Connors' keycard, along with a cloned card. Jack snatched up the card and they hurried through the building.

A few minutes later, they were outside and able to get through the security checkpoint using the access card.

Jack ran over to the truck. He opened the door and stepped up into the cab. He pulled down the visor, catching the ignition key in his hand.

He jumped down, running to the back of the truck. He raised the rear door.

Lennie looked inside the dark cargo hold.

"Don't just stand there, get in."

The yeren huffed.

"You want to see Nora, don't you?"

Lennie's eyes beamed at the mention of her name.

"Then get in, you big lug."

Lennie climbed in, the rear shock absorbers sagging under his massive weight.

Jack yanked down the rear door.

He raced back, got inside the cab, and started the engine.

After seeing the TV broadcast, Jack had a pretty good idea where Nora might be.

Now if he could figure out how to rescue her.

31

NOT AGAIN

Maria went out through the front door and carried the garbage round to the back of the house. She could hear Miguel in the shed, running the table saw. She opened the trash bin by the back porch and dumped the bag inside.

Miguel came out of the shed with the new door. He laid it on two sawhorses he had set up by the porch steps.

"I thought Bron was going to give you a hand with that?" Maria asked.

"He went out with Abe and a group of hunters to look for the bear."

"Shouldn't you have gone with them?"

"They'll call me if they need me. Or would you rather I not fix the door?"

"Yes, I want you to fix the door. Can I help?"

"Sure. You can hold the plywood while I take out the screws." Miguel grabbed his battery-operated screwdriver. Maria stood in front of the plywood sheet covering the rear doorway and held it in place while Miguel went around and removed the screws. He grabbed the upright edges with both hands. He carried the sheet of plywood down the steps and across the yard to the shed. He returned with precut strips of wood for repairing the doorjambs, threshold, and header.

Working together, Maria held the replacement pieces in place, while Miguel either screwed or hammered the sections onto the framework. Miguel chiseled the doorjamb for the hinges. He handed the box of hardware to Maria. "If you want to put these on, I'll prep the door."

"Sure thing, boss."

"Wait, I thought you were the boss," Miguel said.

"You're learning." Maria hip bumped him.

He teetered back, almost falling down the stairs. "Easy there..."

"What were you going to say?"

Miguel pinched a thumb and forefinger together and made a gesture across his lips.

"You better zip it," she said with a grin. She took out a hinge and marked the holes on the doorjamb with a carpenter's pencil. She glanced over at Miguel. He was drilling two holes in the door with a large jig.

Maria used the screwdriver and fastened the hinges to the doorframe.

Together, they hung the door. Miguel installed the doorknob and deadbolt on the door. He finished up screwing in the strike plates on the doorjamb. They stepped back to inspect their work.

"Well, what do you think?" Miguel said.

Maria grabbed the doorknob and opened the door. She gave it a few swings back and forth. "I like it."

"Not too shabby for a couple of amateurs." Miguel stepped through. "Let's test the locks."

Maria followed him inside and she closed the door. She pushed the button on the doorknob and twisted the lever on the deadbolt. She tried opening the door and it held firm. "Works like a charm."

"Great, looks like we're done."

Maria unlocked the door and pulled it towards her.

A giant bigfoot stood on the porch. It was filthy and stunk. Its right eye was gray and squashed in the socket.

"Oh my God," Maria screamed, realizing that it was the same creature Miguel had partially blinded when it invaded their home. Which meant it had a grudge to settle. She shoved the door forward.

The bigfoot's fist blasted through the door, nearly striking Maria in the face, and ripped the door from its hinges. The creature spun, hurling the door across the yard.

The doorway was too short and narrow for the eight-foot tall bigfoot to fit through so it slammed its fist against the outside wall, knocking out chunks of plasterboard. It smashed the top of the doorway splintering the thick header, knocking the shotgun off the wall and sending it clattering onto the kitchen floor.

Maria watched Miguel snatch the weapon. He aimed the barrel at the creature and pulled the trigger but nothing happened as it was against house rules to have a loaded firearm in the house. Miguel searched frantically in his pockets for a loose cartridge.

The bigfoot smashed through the wall. It backhanded the kitchen table, sending it crashing against the counter.

Maria reached back and felt a short stack of dinner plates. She grabbed the top plate. She looked down and saw it was a piece of china from her mother's set. "I'm sorry, Mom." She gripped the porcelain disc like a Frisbee and flung it at the bigfoot's head.

The edge of the plate struck the bigfoot in the forehead and bounced off the creature's thick skull.

She grabbed another plate and sent it flying. "Get the hell out of my kitchen," she screamed.

Miguel had moved to the counter and was rifling through a drawer. He found a shell, and shoved it in the chamber.

The bigfoot lunged just as Miguel fired, blasting a ragged hole in the creature's chest. It bellowed and stumbled back, crashing through the ravaged doorway and tumbled down the steps, landing on its back. Blood bubbled and spurted out of the raw wound, the heavy-load buckshot having pulverized the animal's heart.

Miguel lowered the gun muzzle and turned to Maria. "Are you okay?"

"I can't believe it."

They stared at the massive hole in the kitchen wall.

"All our hard work, ruined just like that."

32

ROOM WITH A VIEW

Nora could tell the creature pacing continuously up and down the opposite side of the glass wall fascinated Laney.

"You're sure it's not a panther?" Laney asked. "It sure looks like one to me."

"Believe me, it's not."

"Then what is it?"

"It's a mngwa."

"A what?"

"It's a giant feline from Tanzania."

"Really? I never heard of it before," Laney said. "Here it comes again."

The big cat prowled alongside the glass barrier like a sentry, its powerful muscles undulating under the dark ebony fur. It stopped to stare at Nora with menacing jade eyes; mouth slightly agape, the tips of its white fangs jutting from its black gums.

"Why does it keep stopping to look at you?" Laney asked.

Nora placed the palm of her hand onto the windowpane divider.

"Nora, what are you doing?"

The mngwa ran its tongue up the glass like it was licking Nora's hand.

"Oh my God. It knows you?"

"It should, I helped create it. It's one of our cryptids. Last time I saw it, it was no bigger than a kitten."

"When was that?"

"Six months ago," Nora said.

"And now it's fully grown?"

Nora laughed, "Hardly. This mngwa weighs maybe 200 pounds and is still an infant. Once it reaches adulthood, it will weigh 1200 pounds and be as tall as a mule."

"That's..."

"Incredible, I know."

They heard a noise that sounded like a pneumatic door opening at the entrance of a supermarket.

"What was that?" Laney asked.

They crept through the dark room and found a glass door standing wide open. Overhead lights automatically came on as soon as they stepped through the opening.

Nora recognized the floor layout the moment she entered the basketball court-sized room with a twenty-foot tall ceiling. The surrounding wall was concave, constructed of dark tinted glass. The ebony marble flooring glistened like an ominous pool from the sunlight shining through a massive floor-to-ceiling observation window.

Steps led up to an ornate throne-like chair facing a panoramic view of dense clouds with patches of blue sky.

Nora and Laney approached the wall. A ten-foot wide section lit up, revealing a jungle setting recessed behind the thick glass. A 200-pound blue tiger cub bounded out of the green foliage. When the large cat saw Nora, it padded over.

Nora put her palm on the glass.

The cub licked the glass the same way as the mngwa. Even though the creatures were conceived in a laboratory, they still yearned for maternal affection.

Nora walked over to a divider strip at the edge of the tiger cub's enclosure.

Another exhibit lit up. A wintry setting with artificial snow on the ground; the entrance to a cave formed inside a manmade igloo. A yeti youngster as tall as Nora stood in the dark archway.

Laney went over to a desert scene with sand and cacti. Four adolescent chupacabras skulked between fake rocks and artificial bushes like a band of grave robbers sneaking through a cemetery.

In a low-ceiling aviary, two molting ostrich-sized thunderbird chicks perched on a rock, their shed feathers on the floor covered with splashed guano.

A young 300 pound bigfoot peered from behind an artificial tree in a redwood forest setting.

Two oblivious, long-necked sauropods grazed on moss grass in the next habitat.

In the last enclosure was the biggest beast of all—the Bergman's bear cub which when it saw Nora staring at it through the glass, stood up on its hind legs. The animal was almost eight feet tall. It sat back down on the floor and rolled around the floor in a playful mood.

Nora gazed at the juvenile creatures, realizing they were the same ones that had mysteriously disappeared after being transported from the airport.

"Isn't it magnificent?" The voice came from the throne-style chair positioned in front of the observation window.

Nora and Laney climbed warily up the steps.

Carter Wilde stared pensively out the massive window.

The few times Nora had ever seen the eccentric billionaire, he was always impeccably dressed in three-piece tailored suits, his silver hair and goatee neatly trimmed.

She was surprised to see him in a black cassock and black boots. He'd grown a full beard and his hair was much longer, pulled back into a ponytail over the nape of his neck.

He looked like a clergyman meditating before a service.

Wilde cocked his head in her direction then motioned to the white cottony clouds outside as though they were his creations. "This is as close to heaven as you'll ever get."

Nora wasn't surprised the eccentric billionaire had developed a God complex with all his power and money. "What have you done with Jack and Lennie?"

"Who's Lennie?"

"My yeren."

"*Your* yeren? Let me remind you who pays the bills here and owns the patents to all your work. Which makes the yeren *my* property. Not yours. As for Mr. Tremens, he's been permanently detained. I don't think you two will be seeing each other anytime soon."

"You'll never get away with this."

"Oh, and who is going to stop me?"

Laney took a step toward Wilde.

"Don't be fooled by the robe." Wilde slipped his hand in his side pocket.

Nora grabbed Laney by the arm, halting her advance.

Laney glared at the man in the chair. "You're going to pay for killing my husband; no one's above the law."

"Is that right?" Wilde said. "If I'm not mistaken, it was you and that husband of yours that broke the law when you vandalized my logging equipment."

"You were destroying the rainforest."

"Think what you may, but that little stunt cost me two and a half million dollars."

"Serves you right, you greedy bastard," Laney growled.

"Say what you may, but a man's worth is his wealth."

"Where did you come up with that gem, a fortune cookie?"

"No, those were my father's words." Wilde stood and opened his arms wide like Moses about to part the Red Sea.

He put his arms down and turned to gaze at the cryptids in the transparent habitats. "As a young boy, my mother would read me stories about strange beasts that lived in the woods, legends and fables mostly as they were my favorites. I would often lie in bed wondering what it would be like if the creatures in those books were real."

He turned to Nora. "And now thanks to you, they really exist. Which is one reason, after some deliberation, I have decided to reconsider your termination. I have big plans for you, Professor Howard."

"And what happens to me?" Laney asked.

"How about I give you the opportunity to work off that money you owe me? What would you say to fifty cents an hour making shoes in one of my Indonesian sweatshops?"

"Go to hell."

Nora glanced out the observation window and felt a wave of vertigo wash over her when she looked down through a break in the cloud cover. The streets below were thin lines, the buildings so tiny the view looked like an aerial shot of a movie set diorama.

Seeing the cityscape from this altitude amid the low-hanging clouds made her feel as though she were adrift in a blimp instead of on the top floor of a towering skyscraper.

Carter Wilde grinned. "Now if you'll excuse me, I have pressing matters to attend to." He walked across the room to a touch pad on the wall. Once he pressed in a code a pocket door slid open.

He stepped through.

The door closed behind him.

"What do we do now?" Laney asked, twirling the hemp bracelet on her wrist nervously like she was rubbing a worry stone.

"I guess we wait and see what happens." Nora looked down at the cryptids staring up at her from their habitats.

She was beginning to sense what a caged animal felt like, her freedom suddenly taken away and trapped with no hope of escaping.

33

HOGWILD

Toby navigated through the bustling city streets. He'd never seen so many cars and delivery trucks in his life, inching along, bumper-to-bumper. Why anyone would want to live in this ant farm was beyond him.

The driver of the car in front had his head down and wasn't paying attention when the traffic began to flow. "Get off your damn phone," Toby yelled. Instead of honking his horn, Toby revved the Barracuda's beefy engine. The loud rumble startled the driver and he caught up to the next vehicle.

"Hang a right at the next light," Allen instructed from the backseat.

"Aye, aye," Toby replied. He glanced over at Alice. She was having a grand time with the top down, watching the pedestrians.

Toby put his blinker on and turned down another congested street. White wooden barriers prevented traffic from going down the next through street. "Which way, left or right?"

"We have to find a way around this," Allen said. "I'm sensing Laney isn't much further." He had on a sweatshirt and some gym clothes of Toby's and was sitting with his arms stretched out along the seatback, his head cocked back so his emerald face could soak up the spotty sunlight shining between the tall buildings.

Toby noticed a strong police presence in the area, squad cars blocking the streets, officers armed with assault rifles. "I wonder what this is all about?"

"Maybe the president's in town," Alice said.

Allen sat forward, placing his green hands on Toby's headrest. "What's that ahead, to the left?"

"Looks like a back alley. You want me to turn?"

"Yeah, follow it up. Maybe we can get a view of what's going on."

Toby edged out of his lane. He waited for a garbage truck to pass then cut across into the alleyway. The narrow thoroughfare sloped upward behind garages below a long string of two-story houses butted together.

The Barracuda barreled up the alley, the dual mufflers reverberating like rumbling thunder.

As soon as they came out onto the next street, Toby turned. He pulled over to the curb. He slipped the shifter into neutral, set the emergency brake, and shut off the engine.

"Wow, will you look at that." He couldn't believe the size of the skyscraper. The towering structure's foundation took up an entire city block. The exterior glass reflected the images of the surrounding buildings. He spotted an observation deck extension two-thirds of the way up. The spire tapered up into the sky like a pyramid, piercing the underbelly of clouds.

Toby saw a massive yellow ribbon stretched across the front entrance.

A huge pair of scissors that looked like it had been confiscated from a giant's sewing box and would take at least two people to carry and operate was propped against a table on a grand stage. A banner—WELCOME TO WILDE SKYWAY—stretched across the top of the platform.

"Looks like a ribbon cutting ceremony," Alice said.

"So that's what all the hoopla is about," Toby said. "I heard on the news this just became the tallest building in the world."

Over a thousand people clustered together, some spilling out into the vacated street, waiting for a speaker to take the podium. A group of protestors was standing behind a barrier, holding signs and ranting against Wilde Enterprises.

Security guards and police working crowd control were positioned everywhere.

Toby glanced over his shoulder. "So what's your spider-plant senses telling you?"

"I know where Laney is," Allen said.

"Great. Which way?" Toby reached to restart the car.

Allen gazed up at the Wilde Skyway structure. "She's up there."

"Ah jeez," Toby said. "So, now what?"

"Being a grand opening, shouldn't it be open to the public?" Alice asked.

"I doubt if we'll be able to get in. Everyone probably had to purchase admission tickets. Plus look at all that security. We're going to need a diversion if we're going to sneak in."

"I know," Toby said. "How about I work my way up to the stage and cause a scene?"

"You'd only get arrested."

"Yeah, scratch that."

"I could pretend to faint. That might do it," Alice said.

"No, you might get hurt." Toby turned to see if Allen had a plan but he had already vaulted out of the car and was standing on the sidewalk.

Allen had his hood up to conceal his face. "I'm going to have to wing it. I'm sure once I get down there something will come to mind."

"I'm coming with you," Alice said.

"Yeah, we didn't come this far to sit on the sidelines," Toby said.

"It's better if you guys stay here."

"The heck you say." Alice opened her door.

Toby got out and hustled to the other side of the car. He tucked Alice's hand inside the crook of his arm and closed the passenger-side door. He smiled at Allen. "Looks like you're outvoted."

"So it does."

They marched down the sidewalk to the corner. More temporary barrier fences were set up along with orange cones in the street reserving a lane for emergency vehicles.

Toby was about to step off the curb when he heard a truck approaching. A white moving van drove past with *Wilde Enterprises* on the side. It turned and disappeared into the Wilde Skyway underground parking lot. A similar vehicle sped by and drove down the ramp.

A third moving van came down the street but instead of following the others, it pulled close to the curb, smashing over the cones and flattened them under its tires.

"What's with this jerk?" Toby said, figuring the driver had run purposely over the cones. A guy jumped out from the passenger-side. He wore an orange jumpsuit like the other two men in the cab.

"Oh my God," Alice said. "You don't think he escaped from jail?"

"He definitely looks like a con." Toby looked at Allen. "You don't think it's some kind of terrorist thing?"

"Let's hope not."

The convict rushed to the rear of the van. He unlocked the latch and pushed up the cargo door. He dashed back and clambered into the cab.

Toby heard a horrendous squeal inside the cargo hold. "What the hell was that?"

Two cops standing a few yards away had seen the man in prison garb get into the moving van and approached with their guns drawn.

The driver rolled down his window and yelled. "Hey pigs! Say hello to our little friend...Hogzilla!"

Before the officers could level their guns, the convict tromped on the gas the exact moment a monstrous beast catapulted out of the back of the van and onto the pavement.

Toby thought he was seeing things. It was like something straight out of a Roger Corman horror movie. The giant pig had large tusks and was the size of a rhinoceros. It reared its head and let out a shrill squeal. Stomping its front hooves, the pig snorted like a locomotive engine building steam.

Spectators standing at the back of the congregation heard the animal and turned, a few screaming as they pushed their way back into the crowd.

The hellish hog charged into the assemblage, bulldozing a wedge like an icebreaker ship cutting a path through a frozen sea. It tossed its head side to side, goring everyone in its path, its heavy hooves trampling over bodies.

Security guards and police officers ran into the fracas.

Toby heard short bursts of gunfire and more people screaming. He could see the swine's shoulders and back bowling through the heads in the crowd. The wild boar crashed into the stage collapsing the platform and tearing down the banner. More shots rang out.

Toby looked over at Allen. "Is that enough of a diversion for you?"

34

DEMOLITION CREW

When Jack pulled the van into the cordoned-off street he immediately hit the brakes when he saw people running in all directions. Many were screaming, some with torn clothes covered in blood. His first thought was a terrorist attack as he could hear gunshots. He saw uniformed police officers with their guns drawn, scrambling against the flow of fleeing people. The first responders raced toward the chaotic epicenter somewhere near the front entrance.

He gazed up at the towering building stretching up into the cloud shrouded sky, dwarfing the rest of the cityscape, then drove at a crawl hoping to spot the other vans.

After leaving the prison, he'd managed to catch up to McCabe's caravan on the freeway following it into the city. But at the last turn he'd lost sight of the vehicles.

He heard a barrage of gunfire and glanced out his side window.

Something struck the front of the van.

Jack slammed on the brakes.

An elderly couple stood on the sidewalk, staring down at the pavement with startled looks on their faces.

Jack put the moving van in park. He threw open his door and jumped down. He saw a person in a hooded sweatshirt and athletic pants lying under the bumper. "Oh my God, are you okay?" He knelt beside the still body.

"Jack, is that you?" a familiar voice asked.

"Allen Moss?" It had been almost two years since Jack had seen the strange man with the bizarre ability to mimic and communicate with species of the plant world. "We thought you and Laney were dead," Jack said, recalling the last time he saw them they were running back into the jungle to escape the clutches of Connors' commandos. "How in the world did you survive the volcano? Miguel and I were in the helicopter and watched the island sink into the ocean."

"I'll tell you later." Allen sat up and struggled to his feet. He pulled back his hood and gazed up at the thin rays of sun slanting down through the clouds. His facial pigment was a lime shade as the chlorophyll levels in his body were depleting from lack of sunlight. "I really need to get out of these clothes."

They turned to the sound of more gunfire. Police officers stepped over dead bodies lying on the promenade, converging on what appeared to be a gigantic pig. Even though its coat was covered with blood and riddled with bullet holes, the creature remained on its feet. With a powerful lunge, it rammed through the glass facade into the ground level of the colossal building.

"How are we going to get inside with that thing running around?" the elderly man said.

"I'm sorry, you know Allen?" Jack asked.

"They drove me," Allen said. "This is Toby and Alice."

"But why are you all here?"

"We've been following Laney's trail," Alice said.

"Allen thinks she's being held captive in that building," Toby chimed in.

Jack gazed up at the skyscraper. "My girlfriend might be in there as well."

Toby spotted the logo on the side of the moving van and turned to Jack. "Three other vans like yours headed down into the underground parking lot."

"Then we better go. Come on, Allen."

"What about us?" Alice asked.

"You better stay here. I'm afraid you'd only slow us down." Jack got in the cab.

"He's right, it's much too dangerous," Allen said, climbing in the passenger-side of the moving van.

Jack glanced out the windshield at the elderly couple. He could tell by their dejected faces he'd hurt their feelings but it was best they remain behind, as they were certainly no match against hardcore criminals.

He gunned the vehicle down the street, making a hard turn and barreled down the ramp into the immense underground parking garage. He cut a beeline across the empty lot, racing between two rows of stanchions then slowed down and stopped when he spotted the three moving vans parked at the loading docks with half a dozen elevators accessing the building.

"Who are they?" Allen asked, pulling off his sweatshirt.

Jack watched the men milling about the trucks. "The one in the white lab coat is Dr. Joel McCabe. He was the head geneticist at the zoo. The others in the orange jump suits are inmates from Stoneham Correctional Facility, a prison owned by Carter Wilde."

"The man behind Wilde Enterprises."

"That's right."

"And what are those things?"

McCabe and an inmate were using handheld tablets to control the movements of two gigantic creatures lumbering onto a loading dock.

"Ah man, this isn't good. They brought the Ozark howlers."

"They look pretty vicious."

"They are. I've seen what they can do."

Jack counted seven convicts armed with riot shotguns confiscated from the prison guards.

Allen raised his rump. He pulled his sweatpants all the way down and slipped them off his feet. He sat back in the seat, completely naked. His body was an olive green and looked like closely trimmed sod. "Ah, much better."

Jack looked him in the face. "Really, you're doing that now?"

"Sorry, but I need my body to breathe."

"What about that?" Jack averted his eyes and jabbed a thumb at Allen's crotch.

"Oh for crying out loud." Allen fiddled for a moment. "There, is that better?"

Jack hesitated then looked down. "Seriously, a fig leaf?"

"Hey, it's the best I can do on short notice," Allen grinned.

"Yeah, well—"

A hole punched through the windshield on the passenger-side, pellets and glass peppering Allen's face and chest. The splatter on the metal wall behind the seat looked like pureed seaweed.

Jack dove onto the seat as a blast blew out the windshield over the steering wheel. Glass rained down on his head and back. Two more shots were fired into the cab.

The barrage puckered the panel behind the bench seat.

Lennie yowled from the cargo hold.

Allen slumped against the armrest and groaned, "Feel like a vegetarian took a big bite out of my head." His molecular restoration worked frantically to repair the damage but the process was painfully slow as his reserves were low.

Jack heard the gunman approaching, ratcheting a shell into the chamber.

They had only seconds before...

A thunderous engine roared in the cavernous garage followed by a heavy thud and a screech of tires. Jack gazed out the pulverized windshield.

A dead convict was on the ground, his gun a few yards away from his body.

Alice gave Jack a friendly wave from the front passenger seat of a pale green convertible.

Toby sat behind the wheel, revving the engine. “So Jack, was that fast enough for you?”

35

SKYWAY

"Is Allen going to be all right?" Alice asked Jack as they headed over to the parked moving vans.

"I think so but we can't wait for him."

McCabe and his band of convicts and the two howlers had already gained access to the building through a service entrance.

Jack bounded up the concrete steps, armed with the dead man's shotgun. Toby and Alice followed him up. Lennie remained at the bottom step and was still tall enough to look Jack straight in the eyes. The animal had bloody patches where he had been struck by the buckshot. He let out a pathetic mewl and dabbed gently at his wounds.

"You coming or what?" Jack said.

Lennie refused to budge from the bottom of the stairs.

"Okay then, you big baby. Wait here."

Jack, Toby, and Alice gathered at the doublewide doorway used for delivering large furniture and bulky equipment. Muffled screams and gunfire could be heard from the other side of the thick metal doors. Jack looked at Toby and Alice. "Stay close and follow me."

"Lead on," Toby said.

Jack pushed through the doors. They scurried down a short hallway to another door, which led out into a lavish lobby with a giant fountain surrounded by Grecian pillars and a grand expanse of marble flooring.

The giant pig was in the fountain and had knocked over the sculptured carp discharging chlorinated water from its mouth. The pool looked like a punchbowl of diluted raspberry Kool-Aid from the profuse amounts of blood oozing out of the monstrous creature's bullet wounds.

Police officers and a SWAT team stood on one side of the fountain, firing their weapons while McCabe's convicts shot back from the opposite side like the feuding Hatfields and McCoys, the shrieking porker caught in the crossfire.

An Ozark howler bolted out from behind a pillar. It attacked a member of the paramilitary unit, severing the man's helmeted head from his body. Two more men fell to the floor, their throats slashed. The officers turned and fired at the howler but it was too swift and bolted for cover behind the ornate columns.

Security guards armed with handguns snuck up on the convicts. The inmate with the handheld tablet spotted them approaching and sicked his howler on them. The men fired a few rounds then fled in different directions, a man falling and screaming as he was disemboweled.

The heavy gunfire continued. A convict took a shot to the head and tumbled into the fountain. Two cops fell to the floor, one managing to crawl for safety. Gun smoke fogged the lobby like a pollution haze from an oil refinery stack.

Jack turned to Toby and nodded toward two separate antechambers leading to the elevators behind the main lobby counter. “You and Alice go to the right and I’ll try the other side.” He waited, and once the couple reached the vestibule, he raced for the other foyer of elevators.

Jack darted around a corner and stopped dead in his tracks.

“How the hell did you get out?” growled Ivan Connors, his pistol leveled at Jack’s chest. “Drop the gun.”

Jack let the shotgun slide from his grip and fall to the floor. “What have you done with Nora?”

“What, you think I’m going to tell you?”

Jack heard something creeping up on him and glanced over his shoulder.

The shaggy howler bared its lower fangs and let out a deep-throated wolf-like growl. Jack moved toward the wall with nowhere to escape. He saw Connors edging toward a freight elevator with its doors standing open.

Jack could feel the howler’s hot breath on his face. He stole a glance at the shotgun on the floor. He knew if he reached for the weapon the howler would rip him to shreds. But what choice did he have? Better to go down fighting than give up.

“Hey! Furball!”

The howler turned to the voice.

“Jack, turn away,” Allen said, balling his hands into fists. He flung out his hands with his fingers extended. A yellowy dust cloud of pollen blew into the howler’s face. The beast withdrew and went into a convulsive sneezing fit, its eyes tearing up.

Jack saw Connors inside the freight elevator. He was stabbing the top button on the panel to get the doors to close. The howler stumbled back into the car as the doors began to shut.

“Get your hands off me you damn...” yelled the convict dangling six feet off the floor by Lennie who had just rounded the corner. The yeren held the man upside down and shook him like he was trying to empty change out of the man's pockets.

Jack caught the tablet from the man's hand and gazed at the screen. He saw Connors cowering in the corner of the elevator car. Connors raised his gun but before he could fire, his image went dark, and a scream came over the tiny speaker.

Lennie released the convict and dropped him on his head.

"Sorry we were late to the party," Allen said.

"Feel free to crash anytime," Jack replied, breathing a sigh of relief.

* * *

Toby kept pressing the up button on the wall. "Come on, will yah." Finally the elevator opened. He nudged Alice inside. The gun battle in the lobby had intensified with bullets zinging everywhere. They moved to the back of the car to escape being hit by a stray bullet. The doors began to close.

A shotgun barrel poked between the doors. A convict in an orange jumpsuit squeezed through. He'd been shot in the right shoulder and left thigh. He limped in, leaned against the stainless steel wall, and aimed the riot gun at Toby and Alice.

"Mind pointing that somewhere else. What, afraid of a couple of old fuddy-duddies?"

Toby felt Alice tug on his sleeve. "Really, old fuddy-duddies?"

"Sorry, I didn't mean it to sound—"

"Shut up! The both of you." By the grimace on the convict's face, Toby could tell he was in a great deal of pain. Which meant he was delirious and wouldn't think twice about pulling the trigger.

Heavy fists pounded on the other side of the elevator doors.

"Get us the hell out of here!" the convict yelled at Toby.

Toby turned to the panel. He saw only one button labeled OD and pushed it.

The elevator began to rise.

"Where will this take us?" Alice asked.

Toby gazed up at the nameplate over the doors. "To the Observation Deck."

"Talk about a shit storm," the convict grumbled. His left leg threatened to buckle as he held onto the railing.

"Well, you jerks started it," Toby reminded the man. "What the hell were you thinking letting those things loose?"

"It was all the damn doctor's idea. He wanted to show off those creatures and scare the hell out of everyone. Ruin Carter Wilde's big day. Payback for getting thrown in prison."

"Well, looks like everything went to plan."

"Shut up, old man."

A loud ding sounded as the elevator came to a stop. The doors opened onto a large sitting room with a string of flat benches and plastic tote bins filled with booty socks.

The convict motioned with his gun for Toby and Alice to get out.

Toby and Alice stepped into the room, triggering an exterior door to open. A gust of wind buffeted them.

"Okay, you two. Out!"

Alice held onto Toby's arm as they stepped out onto a platform jutting fifty feet from the side of the building. The structure was the shape of a giant soap dish with a six-foot tall glass wall running along the perimeter and was shrouded in fog.

Toby looked down through the glass walkway. A wind gust parted the mist for a split second and he almost crapped his pants. The cars below looked like jellybeans.

They had to be 100 floors up.

He could feel Alice shivering from the cold. "We better get back inside."

"No one goes anywhere," the convict said.

Toby glared at the man with the shotgun. "Move out of our way."

"One step and you are dead, old man."

"You won't shoot."

The convict rammed a shell in the chamber. "Oh yeah. Try me."

Toby pulled Alice behind him. "Just put the gun down."

"I warned you." The convict raised the shotgun and aimed at Toby's face.

"Please, don't hurt him," Alice shouted from behind Toby.

Toby took a deep breath and steeled himself.

He heard a loud swoosh.

Enormous bird feet with sharp talons appeared out of the mist, snatched up the convict, and disappeared into the cloud.

Alice peeked around Toby. "Where did he go? Oh my God, did he fall over the railing? That'll teach him for being so mean."

Toby grinned. "Yeah, he did get carried away."

* * *

Nora searched the giant room looking for a way to escape. She'd tried to figure out the code on the push pad that Carter Wilde had used to open the pocket door, but with no success. She thought they might be able to get out through the door in the rear of the habitat they had been kept captive, but it was locked from the other side.

The glass was over two inches thick on the observation window, and even if they could shatter it, there was no way they could climb down the side of the skyscraper.

Two ten-foot tall doors were on the other side of the gymnasium-sized room. Both were locked. Nora had just about given up hope when Laney shouted, "I found something."

Nora hurried over to Laney who was standing in front of a junction box with the door open revealing a breaker panel. Nora saw two rows of black switches, none of them labeled. They were all pointing to the OFF position. She looked at Laney. "They're probably for the lights."

"But the lights are already on," Laney said. "Maybe there's a breaker to open the doors."

Nora gazed over at the twin doors. "It might be a possibility but which one?"

"There's only way to find out." Laney went down the left row, flicking on breaker switches.

"No, no, wait," Nora yelled out.

Laney was already making a pass down the second row. She flicked on the last breaker and turned with a big smile on her face. "There!"

Only Nora wasn't smiling. "I don't think you should have done that."

They both turned around and saw the habitat doors clicking open.

First the blue tiger ventured out, then the giant mwgwa came out cautiously, pacing close to the glass wall. Out followed the bigfoot. The furry humanoid moved slowly, shoulders tense, fists balled at its sides. The six-foot tall yeti came out next. It sized up the other creatures and kept its distance. Then the hideous chupacabras scampered out. They clustered together—strength in numbers—their shoulders hunched, snapping their needle teeth.

Bergman's bear stepped out on all fours, its head down sniffing the floor.

The timid sauropods poked their long necks out but didn't venture from the safety of their containment.

The two ostrich-sized thunderbird chicks jumped out of their habitat and hopped up the steps to the observation window. They flapped their wings excitedly and pecked at the glass when they saw the cloudy sky.

"Looks like I screwed up," Laney said.

Even though the animals kept their distance from each other, they never took their eyes off of Nora. Except for the thunderbird chicks. They were too busy banging on the glass.

The creatures converged on Nora and Laney.

36

LENNIE'S BAPTISM

Jack watched the screen go blank on the tablet. "I've lost the signal." He figured the elevator carrying the Ozark howler—and most likely Ivan Connors' mutilated body—was halfway up the skyscraper. He looked up as a convict rounded the corner. The man spotted him then gawked at the twelve-foot tall yeren and the green man that looked like a zany Jolly Green Giant caricature gleaned from a frozen packet of peas.

The convict pointed his gun.

Allen extended his right arm and a thick white sap shot out of his fingertips. The latex covered the convict's face. Jack thought it looked like a spa treatment until he heard the sizzling and muffled cry. The man clutched his face and tried to tear off the sticky substance and collapsed on the floor. Allen knelt and peeled off the fiery mask. The unconscious man's face was lobster-red with bubbling blisters and had suffered a third-degree burn but at least he was still breathing.

The gunfire out in the lobby sounded more like sporadic shots at a firing range than a law enforcement altercation, which meant there were fewer shooters left standing in the skirmish. Soon more precincts would be answering the call to the strange disturbance at Wilde Skyway's grand opening.

Two police officers backed into the elevator vestibule, unaware that Jack, Allen, and Lennie were there. As soon as they realized there was someone—or some things—standing behind them, the officers turned and pointed their guns.

"Whoa," Jack said, raising his hands. "We're the good guys! Don't shoot!"

"What the hell is that?" the tall cop asked, pointing to the towering yeren.

"Don't worry, Lennie's friendly. He won't hurt you. Just don't point your guns at him."

The officer lowered his weapon. The other cop stared at Allen. "What about...?"

"I'm cool," Allen said, sticking his hands in the air.

Jack could tell the officers were confused, wondering if Allen was just some weirdo in a floral bodysuit or maybe he was a strange alien peace ambassador sent from a distant verdure planet to Earth in hopes of saving the world from self-destruction.

Either way, they gave Allen his space and lowered their weapons.

"How's it going out there?" Jack asked the tall officer.

He hung his head for a moment then looked at Jack. "We lost some good men."

"What about hogzilla?"

"What?"

"The pig."

"The thing was so full of lead, it finally keeled over."

"And the convicts?" Jack asked, cocking his head at the man that Allen had almost suffocated to death, lying on the floor in the orange jumpsuit.

"Our boys got the last two cornered except for the one in the white lab coat. He headed up the stairs with that creature."

"Then we better hit the stairs!" Allen said.

"What, are you crazy?" Jack said. "The stairs? Do you know how tall this building is?"

"Afraid of a little cardio workout?"

"Have a heart."

"Sorry, not part of my molecular makeup." Allen bounded for the nearest door leading to the stairwell.

Jack glanced up at Lennie for a brief second and then faced the two officers. "We should split up and take the elevators."

"We'll get off at the twentieth floor and wait for them there," the tall officer said.

"Sounds like a plan. Lennie and I will go up to the thirtieth floor and cut them off in case they make it past you. Good luck." Jack nudged the big ape-man and they rushed for the freight elevator.

***

When the elevator doors opened on the thirtieth floor, Jack was shocked to find a long rectangular Olympic-sized pool with black lines on the bottom marking the swimming lanes, the overhead lighting refracting in the clear bluish water. A wide walkway edged around the pool, a diving board at the deep end, and chrome handrails for climbing down the metal steps into the shallower side.

Jack heard a door bang open. He turned and saw the howler charge into the massive swimming area. Dr. McCabe rushed in, his eyes glued to the tablet in his hands. He looked up and saw Jack and Lennie standing at the deep end side of the pool. The doctor manipulated his screen and the howler ran down the side of the pool straight for Jack and Lennie. Jack glanced down at the tablet he had confiscated from the convict downstairs. He stared at the screen and could see the image of the howler racing towards him. Jack tapped a button identified simply as SC.

A loud crackle sounded from the howler's shock collar. The animal came to a crashing halt. It shook its head to rid itself of the sudden jolt. It spun around and dashed back toward the doctor.

McCabe operated his tablet and zapped the creature. The howler skidded on the polished floor, lifted its head to the ceiling, and yowled. It turned and bolted back in Jack's direction.

Jack glanced down at his handheld device. He could see the howler advancing on his screen, getting bigger and bigger.

Twenty feet...

Fifteen feet...

Ten feet...

Lennie stepped in front of Jack before he could activate the collar.

The four hundred pound howler rammed full force into the yeren, cutting him off at the knees. Lennie tumbled sideways over the edge and fell into the pool with a big splash.

Jack tapped his finger on the touch device and activated the howler's shock collar.

Again, the creature turned tail back to McCabe.

Allen came in from the stairwell and rushed over to Jack.

Lennie continued to thrash about in the water, slapping his big hands on the surface and kicking his feet, struggling to stay afloat.

"What's wrong with *him*?" Allen asked.

"He can't swim."

"Uh-oh."

The howler was charging back.

Jack glanced down at the tablet. The screen flashed 'Low Battery' then went blank. "No, no, not now!"

"You better get behind me," Allen said.

The howler pounced as Jack ducked behind Allen. It dug in its claws and sank its teeth deep into Allen's body, ready to rip him apart in chunks. But Allen's self-preservation instinct automatically kicked in like it always did whenever he was threatened bodily harm by another entity. His defense mechanism spurred large spikes to jut from his body. The thorny spearheads stabbed into the howler, the tips driving into its head and exiting the creature's skull while explosive gushes of blood burst out of the shaggy beast's back.

Allen withdrew the lethal spines.

The howler smacked to the floor with a heavy thud.

Jack stepped to the edge of the pool and yelled, "Lennie, stand up!"

The yeren continued to flail in the water. His head went under and he came up, gulping in water and gasping for air.

"Damn it, Lennie. Stand!"

Lennie kept slapping the surface, and after much bobbing around, was able to touch the bottom with his toes.

He got his feet under him and managed to stand.

His head and shoulders cleared the water.

The twelve-foot yeren was standing at the deep end—in ten feet of water.

"See, that wasn't so hard," Jack said.

Lennie cuffed the surface with his large palm and splashed Jack.

"Yeah, real funny." Jack turned and looked to the other end of the pool. "Oh, shit."

"What is it?" Allen asked.

"McCabe's gone."

37

CAGE MATCH

Nora heard the twin doors burst open.

"What the hell is that thing?" Laney gasped, staring at the menacing creature standing in the doorway.

"*That* is an Ozark howler." Nora saw an open freight elevator behind the beast and what was left of a body. She saw a decapitated head and instantly recognized the face—Ivan Connors.

The juvenile cryptids turned to face the intruder.

Nora knew the legendary howler was a savage brute as it was on her cryptozoological chart. The only person that could have created such a creature was Dr. Joel McCabe—but that was impossible, he was in prison.

"This is about to get ugly," Nora said.

"Oh boy," Laney said, backing toward the steps leading up to the throne-style chair facing out over the immense observation window where the two thunderbird chicks were still banging on the glass with their beaks.

The two big cats were the first to confront the shaggy beast. They hissed and bared their fangs and seemed a formidable team against the vicious howler.

The bigfoot and yeti were backup defense, shoulders hunched like two burly football players anxious for the play to begin.

Bergman's bear paced back and forth, its eyes never wavering from the monstrosity at the other end of the room.

The cowardly sauropods stayed in their habitat while the chupacabras gathered in a corner, chattering like a bunch of squirrels.

The mngwa leaped in the air and the howler barreled into the room. The invader took a powerful swipe. Four-inch long claws ripped the panther's belly wide open as it sailed over the howler and crashed to the floor in a visceral pool of blood.

Before the blue tiger could pounce, the lightning-fast howler moved in and pinned the big cat to the floor with its powerful paws, biting down on the blue tiger's head and cracking its skull like a walnut.

"Oh my God," Laney said.

Nora and Laney's backs were against the window glass with nowhere to go.

The howler plowed into the yeti sending it flying back into a glass door of a habitat. The yeti hit the floor and tried to get up but fell back down. A large piece of glass had severed the carotid artery in its neck. Bright red blood gushed from the wound, soaking the creature's white fur, and spilt onto the floor.

Rushing in, the bigfoot leaped onto the howler's back like a bull rider, clinging on to avoid the deadly claws. Instead of trying to buck the bigfoot off, the howler charged into the giant bear, knocking it back. The fierce creatures grappled and fought their way up the stairs.

The huge observation window suddenly shattered.

Large sections of glass and metal framing broke away and tumbled out.

Nora and Laney pressed against the wall so as not to be sucked out into the void.

An adult thunderbird hovered outside having smashed the observation window to answer the two chicks' distress calls. The giant bird let out a loud squawk and the young birds dove out the window. They flew into the mist, disappearing inside the cloud.

The howler, bigfoot, and Bergman's bear went sailing out the window.

Nora watched the lighter chupacabras being sucked off their feet and swept out the opening. She heard something give way and looked up.

"Laney, look out!"

A large piece of framing swung down, knocking Nora and Laney out of the skyscraper.

* * *

Jack and Allen rushed out of the elevator as soon as the doors opened. They ran by another elevator. The walls of the car were splattered with blood and the doors kept trying to shut on a human head. Jack turned his attention to the antechamber. The room was extremely cold. Jack could hear wind and saw a large gaping hole in the far wall.

Jack glanced at the gutted mngwa, the blue tiger with its skull crushed, and the yeti lying in a pool of blood. "Looks like Wilde had his own private zoo up here. They must have gotten out and killed each other."

He heard a nasal 'honking' noise. He went over to a habitat and saw the dwarf brontosauruses.

"Are those dinosaurs?" Allen asked.

"Sauropods. Actually, they're called mokele-mbemebe."

"That's a mouthful."

Jack didn't see any sign of Nora and Laney. "They're not here."

"I'm sensing that Laney's somewhere close," Allen said.

"I don't see anyone."

"Trust me. She can't be far."

"How do you know?"

"I can detect the pheromones from Laney's bracelet."

Jack cupped his hand around the sides of his mouth and yelled at the top of his lungs to be heard over the howling wind outside. "LANEY! NORA! CAN YOU HEAR ME?"

He heard a faint cry from outside. He turned to Allen. "Oh my God, did you hear that?" Jack took a step toward the demolished wall and instantly felt his body being pulled forward as if being swept up into the vanes of a jet engine. He stepped back. "If we get too close we'll be sucked out."

"Get behind me and hold onto my shoulders," Allen said.

Allen placed his barefoot on the floor and twisted his instep. He pulled his foot away leaving a sticky residue. "Try and not step where I'm stepping. The sap's like road tar." Allen made sure to keep one foot anchored to the floor to combat the vortex.

Jack held onto Allen like a drunken employee dancing on a conga line at an office party.

The wind became blustery the closer they came to the short flight of stairs.

They fought the gusts and made it up to the top. The wind was howling like the inside of a tornado. Jack could see nothing but clouds. He felt like a parachutist about to jump from a plane.

Allen grabbed the back of the throne-style chair that was bolted to the floor or it would have hurtled out into the white abyss. "Lay flat on the floor."

Jack got down on his belly beside the chair. He looked up and saw Allen swing his body onto the seat. Tendrils grew out of Allen, wrapping around the seatback and harnessing him as though he were in a sport fisherman chair on a charter boat. A long ropey vine magically appeared out of Allen's right wrist and coiled on his lap. He grabbed the end and formed a loop. "Put this around your waist," Allen said, handing Jack the noose.

Jack grabbed the end and rolled onto his back. He pulled the vine over his head and shoulders and cinched it around his midsection. "Now what?"

"Go to the edge and rappel down."

"What?"

"Don't worry, I'll make sure you don't fall."

Jack rolled back onto his stomach. He began inching his way toward the edge. He tried brushing the broken glass out of his way but there was so much it was impossible to clear a path without sharp shards cutting into his palms. He could feel glass grinding into his forearms, stomach, and knees as he dragged himself along the floor like a soldier crawling through a trench of sharp rocks.

By the time he got to the edge, his hands were bleeding and stinging. He looked down and saw the side of the building for only a few feet before the cloudy mist obscured the view. "Can you hear me?" Jack shouted, hoping to be heard over the howling wind.

"Help, we're down here." Jack recognized Nora's voice.

"Are you okay?"

"We're hanging on by a thread."

"Hold on. I'll be right down." Jack turned to Allen who was holding onto Jack's lifeline. He gave Jack the thumbs-up signal.

"Here I come," Jack called down. He slipped his legs over the edge first then let his body slide over. He held onto the vine as Allen slowly lowered him down. Jack could see where the side of the building was scored by fallen debris.

Jack felt a hand on his leg. He looked down and saw Nora and Laney clinging to a bent beam still attached to the side of the building. He could hear the metal creaking from the weight of the two women. It was only a matter of seconds before the entire section broke free.

Careful not to put any added weight on the beam, Jack extended his hand. "I can only take one of you at a time."

"Laney, you go first," Nora said.

"Are you sure?"

"Yes, hurry."

Laney reached out to grab Jack's hand.

The beam shuddered and slipped down six inches.

"There's no time. Both of you! Jump!" Jack shouted.

The women leaped off the beam just as it gave way and plummeted down the side of the building into the mist.

Nora grabbed around Jack's neck, slamming into his body as Laney managed to wrap her arms around his legs. He could feel the vine biting through his waist. He looked up and screamed, "Allen, pull us up!"

But instead of being hoisted by the lifeline, Jack felt them slipping.

"Allen, did you hear me. I said—"

A wave of creeper vines climbed down covering the entire wall. Jack, Nora, and Laney swung over and grabbed the sturdy netting.

Jack felt the lifeline around his waist unravel and fall off. A large object crashed down—the chair Allen had been sitting in—and sailed right past into the mist.

They scaled the vines like boot camp Marines on an exercise course. Allen was waiting when they got to the top. He tethered them with vines and helped them across the room.

"I thought we were goners there," Jack said. "Especially when I saw that chair come at us."

"I couldn't help it," Allen said. "The bolts ripped right out of the floor."

"Couldn't take the weight."

Jack turned and saw Nora and Laney scowling at him. "Sorry, that came out wrong."

Laney gave Allen a big hug. Allen returned the gesture by showering her with tiny rose petals.

"Oh, that's so sweet," Nora said and turned to Jack.

"If you like, I could hit the gift shop."

"Just come here." Nora put her arms around Jack and gave him a big kiss.

"I think it's time we got out of here," Jack said.

"Wait, *where's* Lennie?" Nora asked.

"He's fine." Jack grinned. "He's down at the pool taking a swim."

38

CHANCE DISCOVERY

FBI Special Agent Mark Jennings stepped out of the elevator and found Lucas Finder waiting for him in the large chamber. Jennings took a second to scan the destruction. The glass panels that had been smashed from the giant observation window had been temporarily covered with multiple sheets of plywood. Yellow evidence markers were scattered about the blood-splattered floor, left by the forensic team.

The glass doors had been left open on the empty habitats.

Jennings could only imagine what it must have been like with all of those monsters fighting each other like a scene straight out of a creature-feature horror movie.

"Thank you for meeting me, Mr. Finder," Jennings said.

"I'm here to assist you in any way I can."

"I understand your boss has a secret hideaway up here."

"By 'secret hideaway' I believe you are referring to Carter Wilde's personal suite." Finder glanced over his shoulder and indicated the touch pad next to the pocket door to the right of the observation window.

"That's right. We tried to access the room but couldn't get past the code."

"I'm not surprised. We have the best security that money can buy."

"By the way, where is your boss?"

"He's in Europe. But I'm sure you already know that. I assure you, Carter Wilde has nothing to hide from the authorities."

"Then he won't mind if I snoop around his private suite."

"Do you have a court order?" Finder asked.

"Search warrant's right here," Jennings said, patting the side pocket on his jacket.

"Then I guess it's a moot point. This way." Finder turned and crossed the room with Jennings close behind. They scaled the short flight of stairs to the pocket door.

Finders made a point of blocking Jennings' view so the FBI agent couldn't see the touch pad but he could hear the buttons beep as the code was tapped in.

The pocket door slid open.

Motion detectors automatically triggered the recessed lighting and switched on an array of 50-inch flat screens positioned about the elaborate suite the moment they stepped through the doorway. Jennings felt like he was standing on the trading floor at the New York Stock Exchange as he watched abbreviated company names and stock values scrolling across the bottom of the screens. He recognized CNN on a screen, Fox News on another, covering world events. The sound systems were turned down low to minimize the discordant noise.

Jennings looked around at the lush teak and leather furniture and the gallery of paintings on the walls. An oriental room divider with artwork of a geisha girl separated the living area from what Jennings believed to be the bedroom. A private elevator was next to the wet bar. "Quite the man cave."

"I don't think that's exactly how Mr. Wilde would describe it."

Jennings walked up to the bar and removed a bottle from a shelf. "So what do you think this set him back?"

"I believe that's a bottle of Wray and Nephew Jamaican Rum. Distilled in 1940. I'm thinking that runs about $51,000 dollars."

"Is *that* all?" Jennings put the bottle back on the shelf like he was placing a baby into a bassinette. He turned and saw Finder standing in front of a television, holding a remote control in his hand. Finder was watching an Asian newswoman standing in front of a massive construction site. A split screen image of a skyscraper resembling an African spear piercing the clouds was in the upper left hand corner of the screen.

Finder turned up the sound.

"Well, looks like Saudi Arabia will be crowning its next prince in 2020. Not the next ruler but soon to be the tallest building on the planet. Jeddah Tower. It will be an astounding—*are you ready for this?* —3,732 feet tall. That's 824 feet higher than the newly christened Wilde Skyway. Sorry, Carter Wilde. Better luck next time. This is Jenny Lee, reporting live from Saudi Arabia."

Finder muted the sound.

"Well, looks like the Saudis one-upped your boss," Jennings said.

"Not necessarily."

"How's he going to top that?"

"He has an even better project in mind."

"Oh, and what is that?" Jennings asked.

"Come see for yourself." Finder walked around the geisha girl room divider to what Jennings had thought was the sleeping quarters but turned out to be a small showroom. A model of miniature buildings and structures was displayed on a metal table.

Jennings saw an Eiffel Tower, a pyramid, an Egyptian sphinx, and a blue dome—*Christ almighty, is that a Cryptid Zoo dome?*

"Is he insane?" Jennings said. "Your boss is thinking of building a zoo in Las Vegas? I don't think so."

"No, not there." Finder reached under the lip of the table and pushed a button. The entire table opened up in the center and spread apart in sections. Gears turned and additional pieces rose on mechanical braces to fill in the gaps.

It reminded Jennings of the intricate *Game of Thrones* mobile diorama in the beginning credits of the popular HBO show.

He watched in horror as the layout formed a rough map of Europe and the upper region of Africa.

The icon landmarks that Jennings had mistaken for Las Vegas were now situated in their proper geographic locations—along with five blue domes.

39

SERENITY

Nick and Meg Wells jumped out of the car and raced into the front entrance of Brentwood Meadows psychiatric institute. They could hardly contain their excitement as they scribbled their signatures on the check-in log sheet and pinned on their visitor passes. As soon as they were buzzed through the lobby door, they bolted down the hallway.

Nurse Fleming was waiting by the door to the recreation room.

"Is it true?" Meg asked, unable to stop the flood of tears.

"Yes, last night we had a breakthrough. I was lucky to come into Gabe's room during one of his night terrors. As soon as he woke up, he told me about the nightmare. It's the same recurring nightmare he's been having ever since he's been here. Do you know someone named Shane?"

"Yes, Shane was Gabe's friend. He and his parents went with us on that weekend to Cryptid Zoo. We have no idea what happened to them. They just disappeared without a trace," Nick said.

"Gabe mentioned...a globster?"

"Yeah, it was an exhibit. They called it Patrick. Some weird dead blob thing they claimed washed up on the beach but was still alive."

"That's odd."

"What is?"

"Gabe kept saying it was Shane."

"That's absurd. Why would he say that?" Meg asked.

"Gabe confessed he and Shane snuck out of the hotel you were staying at and went up to that exhibit."

"What?" Nick said.

"Shane got too close to the thing and became infected."

"Oh my God," Meg gasped.

"When they came back to their room Gabe was too ashamed to tell you what happened. The guilt became too much and he completely shut down."

"We had no idea," Meg sobbed.

"I wonder whatever happened to Shane?" Nick asked, knowing it was a rhetorical question.

"Can we see Gabe?" Meg asked.

"Of course." Nurse Fleming consulted her wristwatch. "Dr. Phelps should be available in the next half hour to discuss Gabe's course of outpatient treatments and arrange his release."

"Thank you so much." Meg gave Nurse Fleming a hug.

"Let's not keep our boy waiting," Nick said, pulling Meg gently away.

Nurse Fleming brushed a tear from her cheek. She grabbed her keycard hanging around her neck and swiped the electronic door lock. The door buzzed open.

Gabe was the only one in the room. His head was down, hands flat on the table.

Nick and Meg entered but their son didn't seem to notice.

"Gabe? It's us. Mom and Dad," Meg said.

The young man didn't look up.

"What would you say to coming home?" Nick asked.

Gabe raised his head slowly, his eyes beaming. The corners of his mouth creased his cheeks.

"Thank God," Nick said, smiling at Meg. "I think we have our son back!"

* * *

Miguel spread the hot coals in his brick barbeque with the end of his tongs. Some of the briquettes were starting to turn white which meant it was time to start grilling. "Maria, I think I'm ready if you want to bring out the chicken and steaks."

Maria was laying out paper plates and plastic utensils on one of the picnic tables set up in their backyard for the get-together. "Be right there."

Betsy got up from a bench. "Maria, let me get it."

"Thanks. You'll find everything in the fridge ready to go."

Betsy started for the porch. She passed Bron leaning over an open ice chest, retrieving two bottles of beer. "You know, you could help out."

"I am," Bron said in his defense. "I'm keeping our host hydrated." He backed away with the cold beers held high and sauntered over to Miguel.

Sophia and Tess dashed out from the side of the house. The giggling girls ran up to Abe and Clare's table, and ducked behind the bench.

Sophia looked up at Clare. "We're playing hide and seek from the baby goat."

"Is that right," Clare said with a smile. "I have to warn you the 'kid' can be pretty sneaky."

Tiny hooves suddenly clambered onto the bench. The black and white goat bleated scaring the girls who jumped up and screamed. The young goat leaped off the bench and pranced around the yard, kicking its hind legs in the air like a miniature bucking bronco, its antics drawing laughter from everyone.

The kid ran around the side of the house. Sophia and Tess dashed after it.

Clare glanced under the table. Rounder was lying by her feet, his chin resting on his paws with a pathetic look on his face, too embarrassed to come out and be seen.

"Think he'll ever forgive me?" Abe asked, looking down at the recently shaved dog. The Great Pyrenees looked half the size without all of his hair.

"Let's hope it grows back soon," Clare said. "I don't know if I can take any more of his moping around."

Betsy came out with the platters of meat and brought them over to the barbeque. "Here you go." She put the plates on a cutting board next to the grills.

Miguel took a pull of his beer. "Bron and I were talking about posting something in town to see if we can find homes for the pups."

"What did Gunther and Rosie think of the idea?" Betsy said with a smile.

"I think they're cool with it." Miguel looked over at Bron who was kneeling beside his yellow Lab and Rosie sitting beside the large cardboard box with their puppies.

"Mama!" Sophia screamed.

Everyone turned as Sophia and Tess ran into the backyard. They rushed over to Maria and hid behind her. "What is it, what's wrong?" Maria asked.

"There's a monster!" Tess yelled.

"It took the baby goat!" Sophia shouted, cowering behind her mother.

Heavy footsteps approached.

Sheriff Stone reached for his revolver.

Everyone braced themselves.

A huge beast stomped into the yard. It was carrying the kid.

The sheriff drew his gun.

"Abe, it's okay," Miguel said, stepping between the sheriff and the towering creature.

Jack and Nora came strolling around the corner of the house. They saw everyone staring up at the giant yeren.

"Sorry," Jack said. "We didn't mean to startle everyone. Lennie just wanted to play with the goat." Jack looked up at Lennie. "You better put it down."

Lennie was stroking the goat's head with his forefinger as though it were his pet.

"Lennie!" Nora said firmly.

The yeren huffed then bent down and lowered the goat so that it was standing on the ground. The kid galloped off, kicking its hind legs. It was enough comic relief to get everyone laughing and remove the tension.

Abe holstered his gun.

Miguel and Maria took a moment to hug their friends then introduced Jack and Nora to the Banner family and the Stones as they had never met before.

"Here, let me take over for a bit while you guys catch up," Bron said to Miguel who appreciated the gesture and handed Bron the barbeque tongs.

Miguel went over to the cooler and grabbed a beer for Jack, noticing that Maria was setting Nora up with a glass of wine. He twisted off the cap and handed the bottle to Jack. Miguel waited for Nora to join them before saying, "So, I see you won the custody battle," pointing at Lennie who was standing by the porch.

Nora smiled. "You might say we compromised. It was either that or Wilde was going to be tied up in court facing kidnapping charges."

"I imagine Lennie can be a handful."

"You don't know the half of it," Jack said.

Miguel watched Lennie lumber up the porch stairs. The big lummox was sniffing the back of the house where Miguel had repaired the damage and re-hung a new door for the second time. "What's he doing?"

"He's hunting for something," Jack said.

"Ah jeez," Miguel said. "He's probably picking up traces of that bigfoot that broke into our house."

"Uh-oh," Nora said.

Lennie grabbed the doorknob, and with one powerful yank, ripped the door off its hinges. He turned around still holding the door, a stupefied expression on his face. He looked at Nora like a child that had just broken the cookie jar.

"Oh well," Miguel said resignedly. "Third time's a charm."

* * *

Laney awoke to a loud commotion outside the cottage. She swung her legs off the side of the bed, stuffed her bare feet into her slippers, and grabbed her robe off the hook on the back of the bedroom door. She slipped on her robe and cinched the sash as she shuffled down the hall into the kitchen. Peeking out the window, she saw a heavy-duty vehicle working beyond the trees.

"Allen? What's going on out there?" She waited for Allen to join her in the kitchen but he never appeared. "Allen, where *are* you?"

Figuring he must already be outside, Laney went out the backdoor to see what was going on. She went down the path until she was almost to the clearing. A bulldozer with a heavy metal blade was pushing a large pile of the charred ruins that had once been Allen's greenhouse toward a larger heap. A man operating a tracked loader scooped up a bucketful of debris and spilled it into the back of a dump truck.

She spotted a dual-trailer flatbed big rig parked nearby loaded with building material. A foreman was instructing his small crew who were already staking out the building site.

Laney stepped behind a wintergreen boxwood hedge so the men wouldn't see her in her bathrobe.

"Morning Laney," a woman's voice greeted.

Laney spun around and saw Alice and Toby walking towards her.

"What the heck's going on?" Laney asked.

"Thought you'd be surprised," Toby said with a smile.

"I don't understand, who are all these people?"

"They're here to put up your new greenhouse."

"But how? I never called anyone and we certainly don't have the money to pay for this."

"You needn't worry, dear," Alice chimed in. "It's all been taken care of."

"Please don't tell me you both used your retirement savings."

"Well, not exactly," Toby said. "We started a GoFundMe account at our senior center. News spread fast and the money came pouring in."

"There's going to be a lot of disappointed kids out there wondering where their inheritance went," Alice said with a mischievous grin.

"I don't know what to say." Laney went up to Toby and Alice and gave them big hugs and kisses.

"Hey, I want to get in on this," Allen's voice said and branches shot out from the hedge like the arms of an octopus wrapping around Toby and Alice. They let out gasps when they were given a bit of a playful squeeze. The branches soon released and snapped back into the hedge as

Allen stepped out of the bush. His body was anatomically correct and covered with tiny broad leaves. He looked like a man-sized Chia Pet.

Allen grinned at Toby and Alice as he put his arm around Laney. “Well guys, looks like we’ll soon be back in business!”

The End

TO THE READER

I hope you enjoyed *CRYPTID COUNTRY*. You can learn more about Allen Moss and his wife, Laney and how Jack Tremens and Miguel Walla became cryptid hunters in *CRYPTID ISLAND*, the exciting prequel to *CRYPTID ZOO*.

ACKNOWLEDGEMENTS

I would like to thank Gary Lucas and the wonderful people working with Severed Press that helped with this book. It's truly amazing how folks we may never meet and who live in the most incredible places in the world can truly enrich our lives. Many thanks to Nichola Meaburn for her keen eye. A special thanks to my wonderful daughter and faithful beta reader, Genene Griffiths Ortiz for her enthusiasm and making this so much fun. And of course, I would like to thank you, the reader, for taking the time to share these bizarre and incredible journeys with me.

ABOUT THE AUTHOR

Gerry Griffiths lives in San Jose, California, with his family and their four rescue dogs and a cat. He is a Horror Writers Association member and has over thirty published short stories in various anthologies and magazines, along with a collection entitled *Creatures*. He is also the author of *Silurid*, *The Beasts of Stoneclad Mountain*, *Death Crawlers, Deep in the Jungle*, *The Next World, Battleground Earth*, *Down From Beast Mountain*, *Terror Mountain*, *Cryptid Island (*prequel to *Cryptid Zoo)*, *Cryptid Zoo,* and *Cryptid Country (*sequel to *Cryptid Zoo).*

CHECK OUT OTHER GREAT CRYPTID NOVELS

SWAMP MONSTER MASSACRE
by Hunter Shea

The swamp belongs to them. Humans are only prey. Deep in the overgrown swamps of Florida, where humans rarely dare to enter, lives a race of creatures long thought to be only the stuff of legend. They walk upright but are stronger, taller and more brutal than any man. And when a small boat of tourists, held captive by a fleeing criminal, accidentally kills one of the swamp dwellers' young, the creatures are filled with a terrifyingly human emotion—a merciless lust for vengeance that will paint the trees red with blood.

TERROR MOUNTAIN
by Gerry Griffiths

When Marcus Pike inherits his grandfather's farm and moves his family out to the country, he has no idea there's an unholy terror running rampant about the mountainous farming community. Sheriff Avery Anderson has seen the heinous carnage and the mutilated bodies. He's also seen the giant footprints left in the snow—Bigfoot tracks. Meanwhile, Cole Wagner, and his wife, Kate, are prospecting their gold claim farther up the valley, unaware of the impending dangers lurking in the woods as an early winter storm sets in. Soon the snowy countryside will run red with blood on TERROR MOUNTAIN.

CHECK OUT OTHER GREAT BIGFOOT NOVELS

THE BEASTS OF STONECLAD MOUNTAIN
by Gerry Griffiths

Clay Morgan is overjoyed when he is offered a place to live in a remote wilderness at the base of a notorious mountain. Locals say there are Bigfoot living high up in the dense mountainous forest. Clay is skeptic at first and thinks it's nothing more than tall tales.

But soon Clay becomes a believer when giant creatures invade his new home and snatch his baby boy, Casey.

Now, Clay and his wife, Mia, must rescue their son with the help of Clay's uncle and his dog, a journey up the foreboding mountain that will take them into an unimaginable world...straight into hell!

BIGFOOT AWAKENED
by Alex Laybourne

A weekend away with friends was supposed to be fun. One last chance for Jamie to blow off some steam before she leaves for college, but when the group make a wrong turn, fun is the last thing they find.

From the moment they pass through a small rural town they are being hunted by whatever abominations live in the woods.

Yet, as the beasts attack and the truth is revealed, they learn that despite everything, man still remains the most terrifying evil of them all.

facebook.com/severedpress
twitter.com/severedpress

CHECK OUT OTHER GREAT CRYPTID NOVELS

RETURN TO DYATLOV PASS
by J.H. Moncrieff

In 1959, nine Russian students set off on a skiing expedition in the Ural Mountains. Their mutilated bodies were discovered weeks later. Their bizarre and unexplained deaths are one of the most enduring true mysteries of our time. Nearly sixty years later, podcast host Nat McPherson ventures into the same mountains with her team, determined to finally solve the mystery of the Dyatlov Pass incident. Her plans are thwarted on the first night, when two trackers from her group are brutally slaughtered. The team's guide, a superstitious man from a neighboring village, blames the killings on yetis, but no one believes him. As members of Nat's team die one by one, she must figure out if there's a murderer in their midst—or something even worse—before history repeats itself and her group becomes another casualty of the infamous Dead Mountain.

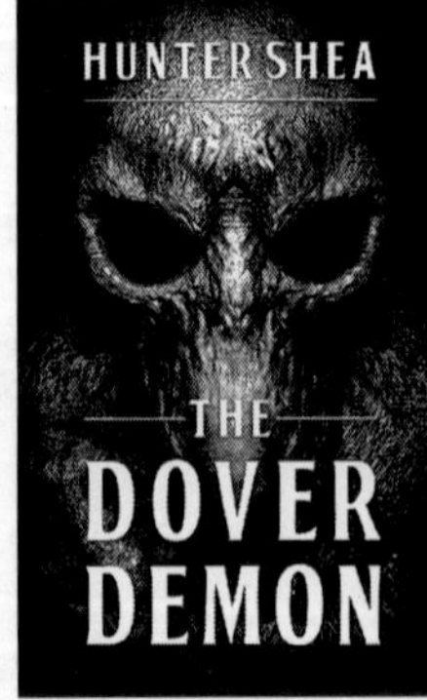

DOVER DEMON
by Hunter Shea

The Dover Demon is real...and it has returned. In 1977, Sam Brogna and his friends came upon a terrifying, alien creature on a deserted country road. What they witnessed was so bizarre, so chilling, they swore their silence. But their lives were changed forever. Decades later, the town of Dover has been hit by a massive blizzard. Sam's son, Nicky, is drawn to search for the infamous cryptid, only to disappear into the bowels of a secret underground lair. The Dover Demon is far deadlier than anyone could have believed. And there are many of them. Can Sam and his reunited friends rescue Nicky and battle a race of creatures so powerful, so sinister, that history itself has been shaped by their secretive presence?